For the Girls of Book Club—YP

For Peyton and Adele—DM

Scholastic Australia
345 Pacific Highway Lindfield NSW 2070
An imprint of Scholastic Australia Pty Limited
PO Box 579 Gosford NSW 2250
ABN 11 000 614 577
www.scholastic.com.au

Part of the Scholastic Group
Sydney · Auckland · New York · Toronto · London · Mexico City
· New Delhi · Hong Kong · Buenos Aires · Puerto Rico

Published by Scholastic Australia in 2016.
Text and illustrations copyright © Scholastic Australia, 2012, 2013.
Text by Yvette Poshoglian.
Cover design, illustrations and inside illustrations by Danielle McDonald.

Cupcake Catastrophe, Best Friend Showdown, Ballet Stars and *The New Girl*
first published by Scholastic Australia in 2012.
Puppy Trouble, The Big Sleepover, Pony Problem and *Cool Kitties*
first published by Scholastic Australia in 2013.

National Library of Australia Cataloguing-in-Publication entry

Creator: Poshoglian, Yvette, author.
Title: Big book of Ella and Olivia / Yvette Poshoglian ; illustrations by Danielle McDonald.
ISBN: 9781760276812 (paperback)
Series: Poshoglian, Yvette. Ella and Olivia.
Subjects: Sisters--Juvenile fiction.
Families--Juvenile fiction.
Friendship--Juvenile fiction.
Other Creators/Contributors: McDonald, Danielle, illustrator.

Dewey Number: A823.4

Typeset in Buccardi

Printed by McPherson's Printing Group, Maryborough, VIC.

Scholastic Australia's policy, in association with McPherson's Printing Group, is to use papers that
are renewable and made efficiently from wood grown in responsibly managed forests, so as to
minimise its environmental footprint.

10 9 8 7 6 5 4 3 2 1   16 17 18 19 20 / 1

By
Yvette Poshoglian

Illustrated by
Danielle McDonald

A Scholastic Australia Book

Contents

Cupcake Catastrophe

By
Yvette Poshoglian

Illustrated by
Danielle McDonald

Chapter One

Ella and Olivia are sisters.
Ella is seven years old.
Olivia is five-and-a-half
years old. They live with
their mum and dad and
little brother Max.

Ella is busy baking. She
is wearing an apron and
holding a wooden spoon.
A packet of flour is open.

There are sprinkles of flour everywhere. Ella doesn't mind getting a little bit messy when she cooks.

Olivia is helping Ella in the kitchen. She helps her big sister with everything! Together they are looking for two mixing bowls. Ella is going to make one mixture. Olivia is going to make another.

There is a recipe book propped up on the counter. It is called *Cupcakes for Princesses*. Mum bought it for them. She thought it would be perfect for *her* little princesses!

Ella and Olivia aren't *real* princesses. But they *are* going to make cupcakes.

Ella has a long ponytail and green eyes. Olivia wears pigtails and has freckles. Her hair is a little bit lighter than Ella's for now. But Olivia hopes it will be the *exact* same shade one day.

The girls' little brother, Max, doesn't have a lot of hair yet.

But when he does, it will probably be the same colour too.

One day, Olivia wants to be just like her big sister. Ella is good at netball and likes to draw. Olivia loves dressing up and pretending to be a fairy princess.

Ella and Olivia both **love** to cook!

Ella and Olivia are very good at helping Mum in the kitchen. Max is also helping. He is sitting on the floor of the kitchen, playing with a wooden spoon and a saucepan. **Bang, crash!** Max likes making noise.

The girls are excited.
They are going to make
cupcakes for Dad. Dad's
birthday party is this
afternoon. Mum bought
a LOT of candles for the
birthday cake.

All the family will be there.
Their cousins Charlie and
Josh are coming. Uncle Stu
and their favourite Aunty
Laura are bringing a big
chocolate cake.

Nanna and Grandad will arrive in their trusty old kombi van.

'What colour icing should we put on the cupcakes?' asks Ella.

Bang, crash, Max answers.

'I like pink,' says Olivia. 'What about you?'

'Ummm,' Ella needs time to think. 'Dad doesn't like pink very much,' Ella says. Then she has a brainwave!

'What about the colours of his favourite footy team?' Ella says.
'Good idea,' says Olivia.

The girls are getting the ingredients ready. Baking is fun, but first you have to make sure you have all the right things to put in the mixture.
'Have we got everything we need?' Ella asks.

Olivia inspects the counter.
There is flour, milk, butter
and eggs.
'Let's start cooking!' says
Olivia.

Chapter Two

The girls are going to make two kinds of cupcakes— orange and brown. Those are the colours of their dad's favourite footy team, the Tigers.

'I love cooking,' Ella says. Ella's favourite things to make include toast and cereal.

'I love cooking too,' says Olivia. Sometimes Olivia helps Mum mash the potatoes in the saucepan. 'One day I want to be a good cook like Mum,' Ella says.

MASH MASH

'What about me?' Dad grumbles. He has crept into the kitchen! 'I can cook, too,' he says. Dad is good at cooking pancakes, schnitzel and eggs. Sometimes Max tries to help him.

But right now Dad should *not* be in here. The cupcakes are a surprise! 'DAD!' cries Ella. 'We told you not to come in!' Ella can be very bossy.

'Out you go,' Mum says.
'OK, OK!' Dad says,
backing out of the kitchen.

Mum is reading another recipe, so together the girls start with their own. They carefully measure the flour and the milk. 'Where's the sugar?' Ella asks Olivia. 'I'll get it!' Olivia says. She hops down from the bench. The kitchen pantry is bulging with all sorts of things.

'Which one is the sugar?' Olivia asks.

'It starts with an 'S',' Ella replies. It's handy to have a kitchen helper like Olivia! Olivia sees the packet that starts with an 'S'. She can tell from the squiggly lines. It's on a high shelf. It has white paper and pink letters. Olivia reaches up on tippy-toes.
'Got it!'
she cries.

The girls measure out the final ingredients and put everything together. They each have their own mixing bowls.

Stir, stir, stir.

The mixtures get nice and thick.

'No glugs and no lumps,' says Ella. That is the secret to good cupcake batter. It has to be smooth.

'No lumps and no glugs,' repeats Olivia. 'Is that what it says in the cookbook?' Ella nods. Mum comes over to inspect their work.
'Well done, girls!' she says. Ella is very excited about the cupcakes. She and Olivia are making them all by themselves—just like big girls! Ella thinks Dad will be very happy.

Mum puts her pretty oven mitts on and checks the temperature of the oven. 'Nearly hot enough,' she tells the girls. 'The next thing you will have to do is put the cupcake mixture into the patty papers,' she says.

Cupcakes are cooked in patty papers, which are placed on a patty pan for baking in the oven.

They have enough room
to make twenty-four
cupcakes.

'I will make twelve orange cupcakes,' says Ella.
'I will make twelve brown cupcakes,' says Olivia.

They must put one neat spoonful of mixture in each patty paper. Mum helps with the first few. 'Just like this,' Mum says. She puts a perfect scoop of batter into the patty paper. 'I hope mine can be as neat as Mum's,' says Ella.

Olivia hopes so too. It takes a few tries. Soon they get the hang of it.

The girls neatly scrape the sides of their bowls. Then they are finished.

Ella and Olivia can't wait for the cupcakes to be ready!

Chapter Three

Mum puts the patty pan into the oven. The timer has been set. Now they have to wait for the cupcake to bake.

Tick-tock.
Tick-tock.

The minutes tick by. Ella looks at her watch.

'How much longer?' asks Ella.

34

'About twenty minutes,' says Mum. 'A watched pot never boils,' she says. Instead, Ella and Olivia help Mum clean up. They clear the counter. They wipe down the mess.

Now they have to make the icing for the cupcakes. Together, they get the next round of ingredients ready for Mum. There is icing sugar, cream cheese, butter and hundreds and thousands.

Ding-a-ling! the oven cries. Mum checks the oven. The cupcakes have risen! They puff up over the patty papers.

'Good girls, Ella and Olivia,' Mum says. 'It looks like you have perfect cupcakes!'

The girls can't wait to see what they look like. Mum takes them out of the oven. She rests them on a rack on the counter. They smell so good. Ella wants to eat one straightaway.

'Don't touch them yet!' Mum warns. 'You might burn your fingers,' she says.

'They're not for you,' Olivia says. 'They are for Dad,' she reminds Ella.

The cupcakes look lovely
and golden on top. They
smell yummy.

'Now we are going to make the icing,' says Mum. Ella fetches another wooden spoon from the drawer for her. Olivia holds up *Cupcakes for Princesses* for Mum. Mum puts on her reading glasses.

'A *bit* of cream cheese . . .' says Mum. Ella hands her the cream cheese. It has gone super soft from sitting on the bench, but that's OK.

'A *lot* of icing sugar,' Mum
says. Olivia hands her the
packet of icing sugar.
'And some butter!'

Mum adds the ingredients
to the bowl. She uses
the electric mixer.
Whirrrrrrrr!
Ella and Olivia watch. Soon
the lumpy, bumpy mixture
turns smooth.
Mum stops to
have a look.

The mixture is a creamy yellow. She takes half of the mixture out and puts it into another bowl.

'One mixture needs to be orange,' says Mum. 'And the other one will be brown.'

Ella is being very careful. She squeezes two drops of orange food dye into one mixture. Then she squeezes two drops of brown food dye into the other.

'Good girl, Ella,' says Mum.
Olivia stirs the mixtures.
One mixture turns orange.
The other turns brown.
'Well done, Olivia,' says
Ella. Little sisters can be
very helpful sometimes!

The guests are nearly here.
The girls put the icing on
the cupcakes and sprinkle
hundreds and thousands
over the top. The cupcakes
look amazing!

'You'd better get ready for the party now, girls!' says Mum.

Ella goes to her bedroom. She knows exactly what she is going to wear. Mum has laid out her favourite lilac dress with white spots.

Ella finds her good shoes in the cupboard. They are shiny patent leather. They have buckles and a very small heel.

Ella goes into the kitchen and does a twirl. Mum is braiding Olivia's hair into a plait. Olivia has a new dress and her favourite shoes on. 'We're ready!' the girls shout together.

Mum claps. 'So are the cupcakes!' she says.

Chapter Four

The girls are nervous and excited. The cupcakes look so pretty. They want Dad to be happy on his birthday. But will the cupcakes taste as good as they look?

Both girls have signed the birthday card. Ella drew it especially for Dad. She loves to draw. Olivia added

a flower and Max drew
a special line in orange
crayon.

'Have you got Dad's
present ready?' Mum asks.
'Yes!' says Ella. She has the
gift in her hands. It is a
joke book. Dad needs some
new jokes. Ella read it first
just in case. She read some
out loud to Olivia too. It is
very funny.

Dad and Max put balloons on the front gate. There is even a sign that says PARTY! The balloons are orange and brown—a perfect match for the cupcakes.

Ella feels very pretty in her dress.
'Hurry up, everyone!' cries Olivia. They can't wait for their cousins to arrive.

The cupcakes look delicious. But before the girls can do a taste test, the doorbell rings.
Ding-dong!
The guests start to arrive! Nanna and Grandad are at the front door.

Grandad is wearing a tropical shirt. Nanna has bright pink earrings on.

'Hello, you two!' They gather the girls into a big hug. Nanna smells like roses. Grandad doesn't.
'We have a secret!' says Ella.
'What is it?' whispers Nanna. She is very good at keeping secrets.
'We made something for Dad,' whispers Olivia.

The girls take Nanna and Grandad by the hand to the kitchen.

'Ooooh!' says Nanna.

'CUPCAKES?' says Grandad, a bit too loudly.

'SHHHHHHHHHHHH!' whisper both girls.

'It's a secret!'

Ding-dong goes the doorbell again. More visitors have arrived!

Olivia runs to open the front door.

'Josh and Charlie!' Ella cries. 'Charlie and Josh!' Olivia cries. Their twin cousins are dressed in matching shirts and shorts. They have sandy-brown hair and freckles. Freckles run in the family.

Soon, everyone is in the kitchen. There are lots of sparkling, fizzy drinks and fruit juices. There are chips and lollies, and a big plate of strawberries and mango. Aunty Laura has hidden the birthday cake in the fridge.

'Guess what we made? Guess! Guess!' Olivia asks Josh. Josh shrugs. He has no idea.

'Ummmm . . .' he says.
'We made delicious
CUPCAKES!' Ella says,
showing her cousins the
tray from behind her back.
The boys lick their lips.
'YUM!' says Josh.
'Did you make them, Ella?'
asks Charlie.
Ella nods. 'Olivia helped
me. So did Mum,' she says.
'I hope you like them!'

Chapter Five

It's time for the party to start. The presents have to be opened! Dad is very excited. He loves birthdays. He tears open wrapping paper and ribbons.
He snorts when he reads his cards.

Dad gets some new socks
and a t-shirt. He even tries
on his new swimming
goggles.

He wears them to unwrap
Ella and Olivia's present.
Dad carefully pulls at the
wrapping paper. Ella isn't
sure Dad can see through
the goggles.
'*100 Jokes for Dad!*' Dad
holds up the present.

Everyone claps. Max burps
loudly. He is excited, too.

Dad opens up the book. He
snorts again.

'What time is it when an elephant sits on your fence?' Dad asks.

Ella knows the answer.
'Ummm . . .' says Grandad.
'Ahhh . . .' says Uncle Stu.
Olivia remembers the answer too. Ella read it to her.
'It's time to get a new fence!' she cries. Then everyone laughs. Dad has a big smile on his face.

Soon it is time to have the birthday cake. And the cupcakes, too!

'We must put the candles on the cake,' Mum says to the girls. It takes a long time! Mum and Aunty Laura light the candles.

Ella and Olivia carry their trays of cupcakes out to the table.

'Happy birthday to you, happy birthday to you,' everyone starts to sing. Dad goes red. He takes a deep breath and blows out the candles. Everyone claps. Mum cuts up the cake.

'Look at you, clever cooks,'
says Dad. His princesses
have made cupcakes. 'Are
the cupcakes for me?' he
asks.
He takes a brown cupcake
and bites into it. Ella waits.
Does it taste good?

Dad's face is a puzzle.
He chews and chews and
chews. *This is not a good
sign*, thinks Ella. Oh dear.
Dad looks confused.

'I think you should try
one,' he whispers to Ella.
Ella picks an orange one.
She bites into it. The icing
is sweet. But the cupcake
is . . . *salty*. She can barely
swallow it. YUCK!

'Uh-oh,' says Mum. She takes a bite.

'I think you might have used salt instead of sugar in the batter.'
Oh no! Ella feels terrible.
This is a cupcake
CATASTROPHE!
Now no-one can eat the pretty cupcakes.

'I can't believe we made salty cupcakes!' Ella says. 'Olivia and I spent so much time baking. We did everything perfectly.'

Then Ella realises. Olivia is still learning to spell. And Ella didn't check the ingredients. That's how the salt was put in instead of the sugar.

'We're so sorry, Dad!' Ella and Olivia say.

'Don't worry,' Dad says.
'You girls are the best. I will
never forget that you made
me something so special!'

Ella and Olivia soon forget
about the cupcakes. There
are more presents to
unwrap and games to play.

Happy birthday, Dad!

Best Friend Showdown

By
Yvette Poshoglian

Illustrated by
Danielle McDonald

Chapter One

Ella and Olivia are sisters. Ella is seven years old. Olivia is five-and-a-half years old. Ella's best friend in the whole world is Zoe. Zoe is also seven.

Ella has green eyes and a fringe. Her brown ponytail swishes at the back. Zoe has black hair and long black eyelashes.

Ella and Zoe do everything together. At school, they sit next to each other. Sometimes they whisper and giggle. Sometimes their teacher, Miss Baker, has to say 'Shhhhhhh'.

They like to play games together at lunchtime. Ella loves netball and Zoe likes to skip. They even eat their sandwiches together.

Ella has a little sister called Olivia and a little brother called Max. Zoe has a big brother called Will and a cat called Bojangles. Ella wishes she could have a pet of her own. Whenever Ella goes to Zoe's house, she likes to find Bojangles and stroke his brown fur. Bojangles doesn't always like this. Sometimes he **meooww̄s** very loudly when Ella pats him.

'I love you, Bojangles,' Ella whispers in his ear.

Zoe thinks Olivia is cute. She has freckles on her nose and wears pigtails. 'I wish I had a little sister! They're cool!' says Zoe.

'No, they're not,' says Ella.
Zoe doesn't know what it's
like to have a little sister.
Olivia is always hanging
around Ella. She is too
young for big school. She
likes to meet Ella and Zoe
at the school gate and
pretend she is a big girl.

Next year Olivia will start
at big school with her sister
and Zoe. She will have
a uniform just her size.

Olivia dreams they will all play together at lunchtime.

Ella and Zoe are sitting together in class on Monday morning. Today, Miss Baker has some news for her students.

'We are going to work on an exciting project, class!' she says.

A project? Ella and Zoe love projects!

'Our school is building a new hall. We need to

raise money to finish the building.'

'How can we help?' asks Zoe. She is curious.

'It involves chocolate,' says Miss Baker.

Chocolate?

How perfect!

'Are you still interested?' their teacher asks.

'YES, MISS BAKER!' the class cries all together.

Chapter Two

'You will all be given a box of chocolates to sell,' says Miss Baker. At the front of the classroom sit twenty-five boxes of chocolates. Each box contains thirty bars. That's a lot of chocolate to sell! Around them, Ella and Zoe's classmates are getting excited. Their friends Peter and Jo are jumping up and down in their seats.

'Yum,' says Zoe, thinking of how many chocolate bars she will eat.

'Can we eat the chocolate?' asks Ella.

'No Ella, you must *sell* the chocolate, not *eat* it,' says Miss Baker.

'I'm going to sell more chocolate bars than anyone!' says Peter loudly.

'Whoever sells the most will get a Gold Star Award,' Miss Baker says.

Ella is already very keen.
She wants a Gold Star
Award.

'I'm going to sell more than
Peter,' she whispers to Zoe.

'No you're not. I'm going
to sell the most chocolate
bars,' Zoe whispers back.

There is a lot of noisy
chatter. Miss Baker has to
settle everyone down.

'Now, now, everyone. The
goal is to sell all of them so
we raise the most money,'

says Miss Baker. 'Make sure you give this letter to your parents,' she says, handing around a note.

But Ella and Zoe think it is a big COMPETITION. They both want the award. Who can sell the most chocolates by the end of the week?

When Ella gets home, her arm is already sore. That chocolate box is heavy! She looks around for Mum and Max but can't see them. She finds Olivia in her bedroom, playing with some dolls.

'Would you like some chocolate, Olivia?' asks Ella.

'YUM! Yes, please!' Olivia cries. 'I love chocolate!'

'That will cost you two dollars,' says Ella.
'I don't have any pocket money left,' grumbles Olivia. It's not fair.
Now she can't have any chocolate.

'I'll make you a deal,' says Ella. 'If you help me sell these chocolates, I will give you a free one.'

'That sounds like a good deal,' says Olivia. She is already rubbing her hands together with glee. Olivia tries to lift the box, but it is too heavy! Instead, she stuffs two bars of chocolate into her pocket. She sets out in search of customers.

'I know, I'll go and find Mummy and Max.'

Ella wants to win. She has to beat Zoe! Now she has Olivia to help her. Even if she is sometimes an annoying little sister, she can still help Ella out.

Mum and Max are digging in the garden. Mum is putting some plants in the ground. Max is making mud pies. *They look like they need chocolate*, thinks Olivia.

'Who would like some
chocolate?' Olivia asks.
Mum turns around, peering
over her sunglasses.

'Where did you get that
chocolate, Olivia?' she asks.
Mummy is curious.
'Ella gave them to
me. I'm helping
her sell them.'
Mummy
frowns and
stands up.

90

She brushes some dirt off her knees. 'I'd better ask Ella what's going on.'
Ella is sitting at her desk in her bedroom. She has taken out all the chocolate bars and counted them. There are twenty-eight bars left to sell. And she can't forget to give one to Olivia. This should be easy! There is a knock at the door.

Knock! Knock!

'Excuse me, Ella,' Mum says.

'Hi, Mum! Would you like to buy some chocolate?' Mum folds her arms over her chest. 'Where did you get all those chocolate bars, Ella?' asks Mum. Ella holds out the note from Miss Baker.

'We're selling chocolates to help raise money for the new school hall,' Ella says.

'Hmmmm,' says Mum. Now

she is smiling. Ella knows
Mum likes chocolate. 'How
much are they?'
'Just two dollars, Mummy!'
she says. 'How
many do you
want?'

Chapter Three

Zoe's house is a hive of activity. Zoe is going to win this competition. She is going to beat Ella! Zoe wants to get the Gold Star Award! She has checked her chocolate stash. She has counted the number of bars. Twice. Zoe has thirty bars to sell in just a week. She'd better hurry if she wants to beat Ella.

Who can Zoe sell her bars
to? She has an idea.

Zoe marches up to her big brother's room. Will is eleven years old. He has black hair like Zoe. It sticks up in funny spikes on top of his head. He likes to play soccer and computer games. Zoe thinks soccer and computer games are boring.

Today, Will is playing on the computer. Zoe knocks loudly on the door.
'Hi, Will,' Zoe says.

'What do you want, Zoe?' Will asks. He doesn't take his eyes off the computer screen. He sighs. Little sisters can be annoying sometimes. They always seem to interrupt in the middle of a game!

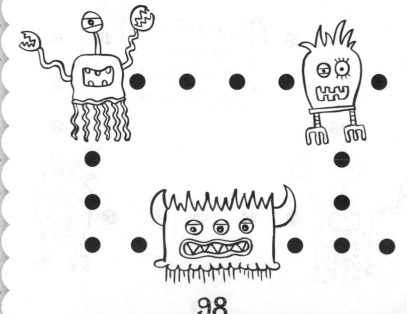

'Do you want some chocolate?' Zoe asks. Will swivels around in his chair. 'Did you say chocolate?' he asks.

Zoe smiles sweetly. 'Yes, Will. It'll cost you just two dollars.'

'Hmmmm,' says Will. 'I don't know if I have any pocket money left.' He stops the computer game. He goes to his sock drawer and pulls out a jar. Yes! Will has found two dollars.

'Here you go, Zoe,' Will says, putting the coins in her hand. She gives him one chocolate bar.

'Thanks, Will!' Zoe says. Will has already opened the chocolate and is eating a piece. Zoe puts the money in her pocket.

Zoe is doing well. She has already sold one of the chocolate bars! She has already made two dollars. There are only twenty-nine bars left to sell. Who else can she sell them to? She sits down to write a list. Zoe tries to think about all the people she knows who might like chocolate.

Zoe writes these names down:

* Mum and Dad

* Grandma

* Mr and Mrs Jones (the neighbours)
* Mr Long (the greengrocer around the corner from our house)

* Ben and James (Will's friends)

Zoe still has a long way to go.

That night, Ella and Zoe
are tired. They have been
thinking a lot about
chocolate. They both
dream about winning the
Gold Star Award.

GOLD
STAR
AWARD

They are pleased with themselves. Zoe has now sold three bars. One to Mummy, one to Daddy and one to Will. Ella has also sold three bars. Mum and Dad bought one each, and even Max bought one—Mum lent him the money! But he is not allowed to eat it yet. Mum put it in the fridge on the top shelf. No-one can reach it there.

Chapter Four

The girls are very busy selling chocolate over the next few days. Zoe has sold a lot! Ella is a teeny, tiny bit worried. Zoe is excited. Mr and Mrs Jones next door bought FIVE chocolate bars. They must **looooove** eating chocolate. She also sold some to Mr Long, the greengrocer. He waggled his finger at her.

'Apples are better for you than chocolate,' he said. He gave Zoe two shiny, red apples to eat.

Ella and Zoe's classmates are selling a lot of chocolate too. Miss Baker is very proud of everyone.

Peter likes bragging about how many he has sold. 'I'm going to win the Gold Star Award,' he tells everyone. He says he has sold nearly all of them! But Zoe and Ella secretly don't believe him. That would be impossible!

Ella is getting a little worried. She hasn't sold very many at all.

'How many have you sold?' asks Zoe. 'I've sold LOTS,' she says. Ella's heart sinks. 'I haven't sold very many,' Ella says with a small voice. She is a bit glum. How is she ever going to sell enough to catch up to Zoe? Zoe is going to win the Gold Star Award after all.

After school on Thursdays, Ella has netball practice. Olivia comes to watch Ella train with the big girls. They pass the ball to each other. Then they practise shooting goals. They wear bibs over their t-shirts so that you can tell what position they play. Olivia can't wait to wear a netball bib and shoot lots of goals when she is a big girl.

Mum, Olivia and Ella head down to the netball courts behind the school. They can see the new school hall being built. There are diggers and bulldozers pushing around big piles of bricks.

Ella leaves her box of chocolates by the side of the courts. She is too busy to sell any more today. *I don't think I'm going to*

win the Gold Star Award,
Ella thinks. Her heart sinks.

The netball team does a
warm-up run. They have
to run two laps of the
oval. The coach blows the
whistle loudly.

'Ready, set . . . GO!' she
says. Ella and the big
girls start running. Soon
Ella forgets all about the
competition.

Mum asks Olivia to play
quietly on the sidelines
while Ella has netball
practice.

Today, Olivia is bored
with her picture books
and fairy wand. Today,
Olivia decides to do
something else. She is
going to help Ella out.
She picks up the box of
chocolates and heads over
to a group of mothers
who are chatting.
'Does anyone want to buy
some chocolate?' Olivia
asks the mums.

Chapter Five

Ella played well at netball today and even scored three goals! But she didn't have time to sell any more chocolates. After dinner, Ella hops into bed. She is a bit sad that she won't win the Gold Star Award.

Olivia is already in her pyjamas. She is sitting on Ella's bed playing with her favourite doll, Miss Sparkle.

'What's the matter, Ella?' asks Olivia. Her big sister seems a bit gloomy.

'I haven't sold enough chocolates this week,' grumbles Ella. 'Zoe has sold nearly *all* of her chocolates!' Olivia smiles a little smile. She has a little secret.

Olivia goes to her room
and hops into bed when
Mum comes in to turn off
the lights. 'Goodnight,
girls,' she says.
Ella is quiet.
'Don't worry,' Olivia
whispers across the dark
hallway. 'It will be OK,' she
says.
But Ella isn't sure. The last
time she looked, her box
was still nearly full.

The next day is Friday. Ella is hoping to win the Gold Star Award today. But Zoe might win it instead. Even though Zoe and Ella are best friends, Ella is a little bit jealous.

Ella has to take the remaining chocolates back to school.

'Here is your chocolate!' says Olivia, holding out the box. When Ella takes 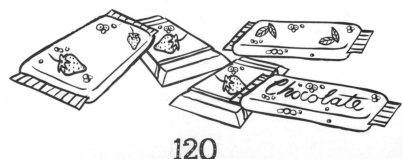 it from her, she gets a surprise. The chocolate box that used to be heavy is really light! She quickly peers inside. There are only five chocolate bars left!

'What did you do?' Ella
asks Olivia.

'I sold the rest for you!'
says Olivia. She is beaming.
She helped her big sister
sell more chocolates!

'When did you do that?'
Ella asks. She can't believe
her good luck!

'While you were playing
netball,' says Olivia. Ella is
so happy and proud of her
little sister.

'You're the best sister in the **WORLD**, Olivia!' she cries.

At school, everyone is nervous. Who has sold the most chocolates?
'And the winner is . . .' says Miss Baker.
Zoe and Ella look at each other. Who is going to win? There is a flutter in Ella's chest.
'Peter!' Miss Baker says.

Zoe and Ella gasp. Peter
has sold TWO whole boxes!
Miss Baker hands Peter the
Gold Star Award. He looks
very proud. Everybody
cheers!

'We couldn't have sold two whole boxes,' whispers Zoe to Ella.

'No way!' whispers Ella to Zoe. They both smile at each other.

'We have two runners-up,'
Miss Baker says.
'What's a runner-up, Miss?'
asks Jo.
'The runner-up is the
person who comes second,'

Miss Baker says. 'We have two second-place prizes.' The class gasps. Who could they be?

'The Silver Star Awards go to . . . Zoe and Ella!' The class claps. 'Zoe and Ella both sold twenty-five bars of chocolate.'

Zoe and Ella are shocked. They tied for second place!

'Well done, girls!' says Miss Baker. She hands them each a very special Silver Star

Award. Everybody crowds around to look. Even Peter is impressed. The awards shine brightly in their hands. It's so exciting to be a runner-up!

'Congratulations to everyone,' Miss Baker says. 'We have raised lots of money to help build the school hall!' Ella and Zoe are very proud.

Ella knows she couldn't have done it without Olivia. Little sisters are cool, just like Zoe said! When Ella gets home, she adds Olivia's name to the award. She does it very carefully, with a silver pen. She slips a bar of chocolate under Olivia's pillow. And together, Ella and Olivia put their Silver Star Award up on the fridge for everyone to see.

Ballet Stars

By
Yvette Poshoglian

Illustrated by
Danielle McDonald

Chapter One

Ella and Olivia are sisters. Ella is seven years old. Olivia is five-and-a-half years old. They live with their mum and dad and little brother Max.

Ella is a ballerina-in-training. She has a tutu, pink ballet shoes and a leotard.

A leotard looks just like
a swimming costume,
but it's not for swimming.
Ballerinas wear them under
their tutus.

Ella has a pink leotard.
The tutu is the fluffy
skirt she wears over it.
Her brown hair is pulled
back into a bun when
she dances. Her fringe is
pinned back so it doesn't
fall in her eyes.

Ella has green eyes. When she dances, her cheeks become as pink as her shoes.

Ella and her friends have their ballet lessons at the Scout Hall. The sign reads:

Mrs Fry's
School of Ballet.

It smells a bit like old socks inside the hall. The Scouts are a messy bunch! Sometimes Mrs Fry burns a sweet-smelling candle to freshen the air.

There are ten students in Mrs Fry's ballet class. To warm up, they all stand at the *barre*.

It is a long rail next to the mirror where they rest their hands. They stand in first position. Then they move into second and third position.

'Girls, we are going to do *pliés* now,' Mrs Fry says. The girls put one hand on the railing. Then they bend and stretch all in a row. Ella loves to *plié*. She can bend her legs very low.

'**Loooooong** stretches,' Mrs Fry says. She stands at the front of the room. She has her own special *barre*. Mrs Fry used to be a ballerina for a ballet

company in the city.
She looks just like a
ballerina. Sometimes she
wears a pink cardigan
around her shoulders to
keep warm. Mummy says
that Mrs Fry looks elegant.

Ella's little sister, Olivia, loves to watch Mrs Fry and the girls. She watches from the back of the hall. Olivia also points her toes and pretends she is on the stage. She is five-and-a-half years old. She has brown hair like Ella and a splash of freckles across her nose. Mummy says she can do ballet too when she is older. Olivia just can't wait!

Olivia and Ella's little brother, Max, is too little to dance. But he is quite good at crawling.

Ballet and crawling aren't the same thing, thinks Olivia.

The girls go through their warm-ups. This is so their muscles don't get sore after dancing. Mrs Fry puts some music on.

'Let's dance, girls!' she says.

Music fills the room. Their feet begin to move. The girls do some *pirouettes,* or twirls. Ella loves to twirl. She can do two in a row without wobbling or falling over.

'Well done, Ella!' Mrs Fry says. 'Hold your head up!' Ella straightens her back. She wants to be a very good dancer.

The girls are learning a new move today called *jeté*. They jump in the air off one foot and land on the other. After they have finished their *jetés*, they cool down.

Mrs Fry gathers everyone
around.

'I have some exciting news,' she says. 'We are going to put on a show!'

There is a loud cheer.

I want to be the star, thinks Ella.

Maybe I could be the star! thinks Olivia. She practises her twirls at the back of the hall.

Chapter Two

'We will be performing
Cinderella,' says Mrs Fry.
The girls chatter away.
Who will be Cinderella?
Ella hopes she will get to
perform a solo! Everyone
will come to watch.

'Everyone will dance and be
a star,' says Mrs Fry gently.
'But only one person can
perform the solo,' she says.

Ella and the girls clap
their hands with glee. Ella
can't wait for Mummy and
Daddy and Olivia and Max
to come to the concert.
'This week, you must
practise very hard,' says
Mrs Fry. 'Next week, I will
choose our soloist.'

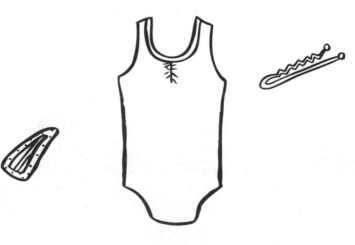

All week, Ella practises ballet at home. She wants to be Cinderella. Ella simply loves ballet. Every day after school, she changes into her special outfit to practise. On goes her leotard. On go her ballet slippers. Ella slides in some hairpins to pull her fringe back.

But Ella doesn't have a *barre* like the one at ballet school. Instead, she uses the towel rail in the bathroom. It is the perfect height. Ella practises her *pliés* in there.

'What are you doing?' Olivia asks Ella.

'Are you dancing in the **BATHROOM**?'

Olivia laughs. She thinks it is the funniest thing she's ever seen.

'If I close my eyes, it's just like ballet school,' Ella says.

'Can I stretch too?' Olivia asks.

'No! There is no room for you,' Ella says. She goes back to practising in front of the mirror. But Olivia wants to dance. She runs to the bedroom.

Olivia digs around in her cupboard until she finds what she is looking for. There it is! She brushes off some sand and puts it on. She finds her favourite shoes and slides her feet into them. Olivia marches into the bathroom. 'I'm ready,' she says.

Now it is Ella's turn to laugh. Olivia is wearing her swimming costume and her sandals! She is a very odd ballerina! Her 'leotard' is blue. It has yellow starfish all over it. It is NOT pink. Her sandals are PURPLE.

'You can't do ballet in your swimmers!' says Ella.
'Yes, I can,' Olivia says.
'Swimmers look exactly like leotards! Watch!'

Olivia goes to the towel rail and stands next to Ella. She bends her knees low, just like Ella does. The swimming costume really is perfect.
'OK, Olivia,' Ella says. 'Follow my lead!'

Chapter Three

The next ballet lesson takes **FOREVER** to arrive. Ella has been practising very hard all week. Olivia has been helping her.

Mummy and Daddy are very proud of their bathroom ballet dancers. Even Max gurgled and clapped when he saw his sisters dancing.

156

Finally, it is the day of the lesson. Mrs Fry puts the music on. Ruby and Chloe and the other girls begin to dance. Maria and Gemma are still warming up.

Ella moves her arms into first, second and third position. Ballerinas are always graceful, with their heads held high.

During class, Ella tries extra hard. She bends super-low. She jumps super-high. She is as graceful as a gazelle. Mrs Fry notices how hard Ella is trying. She thinks Ella is a wonderful dancer.

At the end of the class, Mrs Fry gathers the girls around. They all hope that they will be chosen for the main parts. Ella crosses her fingers and tries to cross her toes.

Mrs Fry has a list in her hand. 'I have chosen Chloe, Ruby and Ella to be the main dancers,' she says. Ella has fluttery butterflies in her tummy.

'Chloe will be Cinderella,' says Mrs Fry. Ella's heart sinks. 'She will have a solo.' Chloe has a big smile on her face.

But what will Ella be?

'Ella and Ruby will be the stepsisters.' Olivia claps loudly. Her sister is going to be a ballet star!

Ella is a bit cross. She doesn't want to be an evil stepsister! The stepsisters are very mean to Cinderella. They make her cook and clean and wear rags.

Ella wants to be Cinderella!
After all, Cinderella goes
to the ball and meets a
handsome prince.
'CinderELLA' even has
the name 'Ella' in it.
Ella stamps her foot and
crosses her arms. Mrs Fry
looks at Ella and frowns.
'What's wrong, Ella?' she
asks.
'Nothing,' Ella says in a very
small voice. But inside she
is grumpy. It is so unfair!

'Alright girls,' Mrs Fry says, 'at our next lesson we will rehearse our special ballet moves.'

The class finishes and Ella stomps off. Mummy and Olivia are a bit confused.

Ella takes off her tutu and throws it on the ground. She pulls off one ballet  slipper at a time.

'Ella!' Mummy says. 'Stop being silly!'

Ella doesn't care. She takes out all the pins in her hair. It springs out from the bun and falls in her face.

'Humphhrphmmmm,' Ella says under her breath.

'Stop acting like a baby,' says Mummy.

'I'm not a **BABY!**' Ella yells at the top of her lungs. Olivia's eyes widen in surprise. What is wrong with Ella?

'I want to be Cinderella!' shouts Ella. 'It's not FAAAAAAAAAAAIR!'

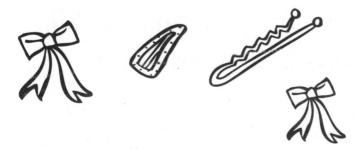

Chapter Four

Ella screws up her face.
'It's not fair, Mummy!' she
wails. Tears roll down her
cheeks.
'Stop it at once!' Mummy
says. Ella is acting like a
spoiled brat.

'But I'm the best dancer in
the class,' Ella cries.

'You still get to dance on stage,' Olivia whispers.

Ella cries even harder.

She cries so hard that her leotard is wet with her tears.

'But I want the ballet solo! I'm CinderELLA!'

Olivia does a twirl. 'You get to be Cinderella's stepsister,' she says. 'How cool is that?'

But Ella can't see how being a stepsister is cool.

'Don't forget that poor Cinderella cleans all day,' Olivia reminds Ella. 'She does all the dirty work. Cinderella washes and dusts. **BORING!**' she says, trying to do a *jeté*. Ella feels a teensy bit better.

Ella watches Olivia. She is doing it all wrong.

'You do a *jeté* like this,'
Ella says. 'Watch me.' She
stands on one foot. She
jumps in the air and lands
on the other foot. Together,
the girls practise their *jetés*.

Olivia loves learning about ballet. Soon Ella forgets about her tantrum. She is too busy showing Olivia how to dance.

At the back of the hall, Mrs Fry watches Ella and Olivia. She has a plan for both of the girls. Mrs Fry thinks she has just the right job for Olivia.

Ella has to practise her part. She will have a special costume for the performance. Her hair will be pulled back in a bun. Mummy even said that she could wear *glitter* on her eyes. That's what ballet dancers wear. Mummy is helping Mrs Fry make the costumes.

'What does mine look like, Mummy?' Ella peers into her mother's bedroom. Mummy is working at her sewing machine. It makes a humming noise. She presses a small pedal on the floor. It starts to hum.

'No peeking, Ella!' Mummy says. Too late. Ella has seen some purple, sparkly material.

I wonder if that is what Cinderella is going to wear, she thinks. Ella's heart sinks.

Ella wishes she could do the ballet solo. Cinderella's costume will be very pretty! And she will be the star of the show.

Later in the week, the girls have their final rehearsal. There is a big poster outside the Scout Hall. It reads:

Mrs Fry's
School of Ballet
presents
Cinderella
this Saturday, 6.30pm.

A group of girls are chatting outside.

'It's so exciting!' says Chloe.

'I can't wait!' says Ruby.

'I wonder what we will wear,' says Ella.

'I wish I could dance, too,' whispers Olivia. But nobody hears her.

Mrs Fry is very pleased. Her little dancers have come along very well. Chloe will be a good Cinderella. Ella and Ruby will be very good stepsisters. She is glad that Ella got over her tantrum.

All the girls are floating on air. They listen closely to

the beautiful music. Some of the music makes them feel sad. Some of the music makes them happy. They move gracefully. Their *jetés* are very high. Their landings are smooth. The big night is only two days away. The lesson is nearly finished. 'You are ready to perform, girls!' says Mrs Fry.

PHEW! They have all practised hard this week.

As they cool down, Mrs Fry finds Olivia and Mummy at the back of the hall.
'I have a very special job for you, Olivia,' she says.

Chapter Five

The big night is finally here. Ella and Olivia arrive at the hall. The Scout Hall has been magically transformed. Fairy lights have been strung around the front door. Inside, the lights are low. The stage is lit. It looks like the inside of a castle—the one where Cinderella lives.

The girls say goodbye to
Max and Daddy.
'See you on the stage, my
superstars!' he says. Max
gives Ella a
sloppy good-
luck kiss.

'Eww, Max. **DROOL!**' she wipes it off. Ballet stars don't have drool on their faces!

Backstage, the air is filled with a buzz. Everyone needs to put on their new costumes and make-up. Leotards are being slipped on and ballet shoes are being wrapped. Some girls are busy warming up at the *barre*.

'Hurry up, everyone,' says
Mrs Fry. 'Ten minutes till
showtime!'
'Oohhhhh,' the girls say.

Mummy has Ella's costume
in a bag. When she pulls
it out, Ella's eyes widen.
It is a sparkly purple tutu!
There is even a sparkly
purple leotard to match.
Hooray!
'Thank you, Mummy,' Ella
says.

'I helped, too,' says Olivia.
'I glued the sparkles on.'

Ella gives Olivia a hug.
'I wish you could dance
tonight, too,' Ella says.

'And here's Olivia's costume,' says Mummy. Olivia has a big smile on her face.

She has her very own white leotard. She has a white tutu as well! No more swimmers for Olivia.

Mrs Fry comes over to inspect the girls.
'Here are your first ballet shoes, Olivia,' she says.

'You should be very proud of your sister, Ella,' says Mrs Fry. 'She has a special job tonight!'

Ella wonders what it is. Is Olivia going to dance?

On the other side of the room, Chloe is getting ready. 'We have to put on our make-up,' she says to Ella.

Together they go over to the mirror. There are pots of potions. There are jars of sparkles. Chloe puts some pink lip gloss on. 'Are you excited?' says Ella.

'Yes! But I wish my costume wasn't brown,' she says.

Ella looks down. Sure enough, Chloe is dressed in rags. It is what Cinderella would have worn. Even her

ballet shoes are brown.
Ella is suddenly very
pleased with her sparkly
purple tutu.

'Two minutes, girls,' Mrs
Fry swoops in. 'Take your
places!'

Behind the curtain, the
girls get ready. The crowd
goes quiet. Ella peeks
around the curtain.

There are lots of people!
Suddenly she gets nervous.

She looks for Mummy,
Daddy and Max in the
crowd. And where did
Olivia disappear to?
The lights go down.
Someone says 'Shhhhhhhh'.
All the girls hold hands in
excitement.

A spotlight comes on.
Ella is surprised. Olivia is
walking across the stage in
her tutu! She holds a sign:

Cinderella
by Mrs Fry's School
of Ballet

The crowd claps. Olivia floats across the stage. Her big job is done.

The music begins. The curtains rise. Ella takes a deep breath. Her heart is

beating fast. Then Ella is on the stage. She is dancing, twirling, **SOARING!** And even though she isn't Cinderella, she is a star.

By
Yvette Poshoglian

Illustrated by
Danielle McDonald

Chapter One

Ella and Olivia are sisters.
Ella is seven years old.
Olivia is five-and-a-half
years old. They live with
their mum and dad and
little brother Max.

Today is a very BIG day
for Ella and Olivia. They
are going to BIG school
together.

Ella is in second grade this year. Her long hair is tied back in a green ribbon. She has lots of friends at school. Ella and her friends like to do ballet and play netball.

It is Olivia's first day at big school. She loves to draw. She could paint all day long. Olivia can't wait to introduce her doll, Miss Sparkle, to some new friends. Maybe they will

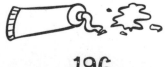

like drawing and
painting too!

The two girls are wearing
the same kind of uniform.
It is purple and pink and
white. Olivia's dress is a bit
long. It hangs down over
her knees.

'You will grow into it in no
time,' says Mummy. Olivia
hopes so. Ella's dress is just
right.

The girls have a little brother called Max. He is learning to walk, but he is still not big enough for school.

Ella loves going to school. She's been at big school for a long time now. She's an expert.

She is going to show Olivia
how everything works.
Everyone has come to
school to wish Olivia good
luck. Mummy, Daddy and
Max are all there.

'This is the front gate, Olivia,' Ella says, pointing to the front gate. 'That is the playground,' she says, pointing to the playground. Olivia nods. She knows all about the gate and the playground. 'Oooh! The slide and the monkey bars!' Olivia says. She has played here before. Olivia used to wait with Mummy or Daddy to pick Ella up after school.

'There is Miss Baker!' Ella says. Miss Baker was Ella's teacher for Year One. The teacher waves to the girls.

Ella points to a big building. 'That's the Year Two classroom. That's where I will have lessons. I will not be very far away from your classroom,' she says.

Ella waves goodbye when Mummy and Daddy take Olivia to meet her new teacher, Miss Kim. Max is busy picking his nose. He is not quite ready for school yet.

Lots of new kids are coming through the gate. They look a bit itchy. **Scratch, scratch.** Their new uniforms are a bit tight or a bit loose or a bit long.

'EXCUSE ME! COMING THROUGH!' says a loud voice. Ella turns to look. The voice belongs to a girl with two black plaits. She has a bright pink backpack and pink hair elastics. Her uniform is a little bit too big. Ella hasn't seen her at school before.

'DOES ANYONE KNOW WHERE THE YEAR TWO CLASSROOM IS?' says a lady next to the girl.

It must be her mum. She is wearing a bright pink jacket. Her lipstick and head band matches the jacket.

'I know where everything is,' Ella says. 'Follow me.'

Ella takes the lead. She is happy to show the new girl around. Ella knows a LOT about her school. The new girl might even be in her class! She might become Ella's new friend. Ella thinks her pink shoelaces are cool.

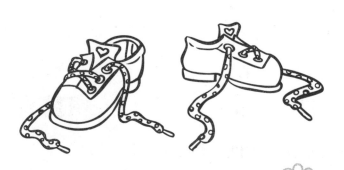

'That building is the library,' says Ella. 'That's the playground, the office . . . and this is the Year Two classroom.'

Behind her, the lady and the girl are whispering. They think Ella can't hear. 'This school doesn't have enough trees,' whispers the mother.
'The playground is TINY,' whispers the girl.

Ella is upset. This new girl is definitely **NOT** going to be Ella's friend. There is nothing wrong at all with her school. *Pink shoelaces are for babies,* thinks Ella.

Chapter Two

Ella's new class this year is 2W. Her new teacher is Mr Williams. He wears a tie that looks like piano keys. He has curly blond hair and a big smile.

Ella sits next to her best friend Zoe. Her friends Peter and Jo are also in 2W. She waves to them as they walk to their desks. Ella looks around at her new home. She is very pleased. Their classroom is on the second floor. From up here, she can see the playground. The walls are bare. The board is clean. The desks are shiny.

There is a knock at the door. 'Who is that?' Zoe whispers to Ella. **OH NO!** It is the new girl. She is standing at the front of the classroom. She still has her pink backpack on.

'She has really cool shoelaces,' Zoe says. 'They're for babies,' whispers Ella. Zoe frowns.

'This is Millie,' says Mr Williams. 'Millie is new to our school. She has just moved here.'
The new girl stares hard at Ella. She doesn't smile at all.

'Welcome, Millie!' says Mr Williams. Everyone claps. Ella claps very quietly. 'There is a spare seat on the other side of Ella, you can sit there,' says Mr Williams.

The new girl rolls her eyes.
So does Ella.

The students take out their
pencil cases and books.
Millie unpacks her bag.

Millie takes out her pencil
case and ruler, her colour
pencils and an eraser. She
places them all in a row on
her desk. Millie looks over
at Ella.

'My stuff is better than
your stuff,' she whispers.

'No, it's not!' Ella whispers back. Ella has a brand-new pencil case with her name on it.

'Shh, please, girls,' says Mr Williams.

Their first lesson is handwriting. Ella has been practising over the holidays. Her handwriting is very neat. She crosses all her Ts and dots all her Is.

Ella looks over at Millie's handwriting. It is a bit different to hers.

'You can't write very well,' says Millie. 'Your page looks messy.'

'No it doesn't!' Ella cries. Millie is being really mean.

'SHH!' says Mr Williams.

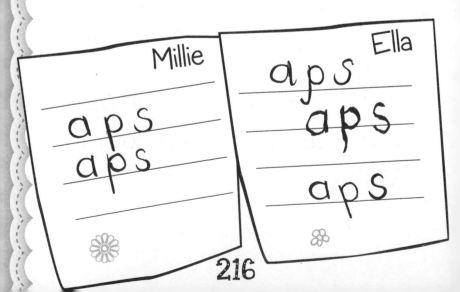

Millie puts up her hand.
'I need to go to the
bathroom,' she says.
'Ella, could you please
show Millie where they
are?' asks Mr Williams.
Ella groans. She doesn't
want to help the new girl.
Mr Williams puts his hands
on his hips. 'Do I have to
ask you twice, Ella?'
'No, Mr Williams,' says
Ella. She sighs. 'Come on,
Millie.'

Millie follows Ella down the hallway.

'My old school was better than this school,' says Millie. 'Our classrooms were bigger.'

'Who cares?' says Ella. 'I don't.' But she does. Millie is annoying.

'I had lots of friends,' says Millie. 'Lots and lots.'

'Well, you can't be my friend,' Ella says. Millie goes quiet.

'Why would I want to be your friend?' Millie says. 'Like I said, I already have lots of friends.'

'Fine!' says Ella.

'Fine!' says Millie.

Chapter Three

The morning passes
quickly. Soon, the lunch
bell rings. Ella and Zoe race
out to the playground. Zoe
has a new skipping rope.
But they must eat their
lunch before playtime.
Today, Zoe has a tuna
sandwich. Ella has a salad-
and-cheese sandwich.
Millie sits on a bench all
by herself.

When Ella isn't looking,
Millie sneaks a glance at
the other girls.

Millie unpacks her lunch box. She doesn't have a tuna or salad sandwich. Millie has sushi. She even has her own set of chopsticks and soy sauce. Millie eats four pieces of sushi with her chopsticks.

She learned to use them when she was just four years old.

I can't use chopsticks, thinks Ella. *My sandwich is a bit plain.* But she doesn't say anything. She doesn't want to talk to Millie at all. There is **NO WAY** she wants to swap her lunch for Millie's.

The playtime bell rings. Zoe and Ella jump up and begin skipping. Peter and Jo come over too. Soon everyone is having fun. Then Ella hears a loud voice say: 'Skipping is **BORING!**'

Of course, it's Millie.

Some of the other kids are watching Millie. She is drawing with a piece of chalk on the ground. First she draws one box. Then she draws another.

'Hopscotch is **SOOO** much better,' says Millie.

Soon, everyone is watching Millie play hopscotch. Peter and Jo go to watch too.

Zoe and Ella are left alone.
They have no-one left to
skip with.

'I hate hopscotch!' Ella says loudly. But Millie and the others don't hear. They are too busy throwing stones onto the squares.

Ella hears another voice calling across the busy playground. It is Olivia! Olivia runs over to Ella and gives her a big hug. Wow! Ella is still surprised to see Olivia in a uniform. Her little sister is growing up!

'I love being at big school!' says Olivia. 'My teacher is so nice. And I've got a new friend called Lily.'

'That's great, Olivia!' But Ella is distracted by what the new girl is doing.

Olivia turns to Zoe, 'Hi, Zoe!' She knows Zoe is Ella's best friend. Zoe thinks Olivia is really cool. She wishes she had a sister. Her brother Will is no fun.

He only likes playing computer games.

'Do you want to play hopscotch?' Zoe asks. 'Come on!'

And just like that, Ella is alone. She still holds the skipping rope. All the other kids are having so much fun playing with Millie. Olivia is finally playing with the big girls. Ella feels a TEENSY bit left out.

Then she hears a very
LOUD voice.

'You're too little to play
hopscotch,' Millie says. 'No
babies allowed!' Ella can't
see who she is talking to.
But then Olivia walks over
to Ella. She holds back
fresh tears.

'I'm not allowed to play,'
Olivia sniffs. 'That girl is
being mean!'

'That's **IT**!' Ella yells.
She doesn't think Millie

should be mean to Olivia.
Besides, Olivia isn't a baby
anymore—she is at big
school!

Ella pushes her way to the
front of the crowd.

'Millie, you're busted!
No-one yells at my little
sister and gets away with it!'

Chapter Four

Ella is upset that Millie
yelled at Olivia.

'Ella is not happy,' says Jo.

'Uh-oh,' says Peter.

'Take my hand, Olivia,'
says Zoe. Olivia scrambles
out of the way. Zoe is just
like another big sister. She
always looks out for Olivia.
Ella looks angry. Millie
looks mean. Everyone
knows there will be a fight.

Ella jabs a finger at Millie.
'You should let Olivia play
if she wants to,' says Ella.
'She's too little,' says Millie.
Her black plaits bounce up
and down.
'NO, SHE'S NOT!' Ella
yells loudly.
'YES, SHE IS!' Millie yells
even louder.

The crowd closes in around
them. Ella and Millie come
face-to-face.

Then, an even louder voice booms out over everyone. 'What is going on here, Ella?' Mr Williams looks angry.

'She started it,' says Ella, pointing at Millie. Mr. Williams looks at Millie. 'Is this true?' he asks. But before anyone says more, the bell rings. Ella is furious. Mr Williams is disappointed.

Although no-one notices, Millie feels frightened and alone on her first day at a new school. It doesn't seem fair, even if she has been a little mean.

Back in the classroom, Millie and Ella sit next to each other again. Ella looks straight ahead. So does Millie. Ella doesn't smile. Millie is very quiet.

'It's story time,' says Mr Williams. 'First we are going to read a story together,' he says. 'Then we are going to write stories about what we did in the holidays.'

'This is so boring!' whispers Millie underneath her breath. She folds her arms.

There are beanbags to sit on at the front of the room. Ella and Zoe share a beanbag.

Mr Williams chooses a
book from the bookshelf.
There are princesses,
dragons and fairies
on the front cover.

Millie sits on her own. She has no-one to share her beanbag with.

'One day in a land far, far away . . .' begins Mr Williams. 'There was a princess named . . .'

'I want to be a princess one day,' Ella whispers to Zoe.

'I want to ride a flying dragon,' says Zoe.

'I want to be a fairy,' whispers Millie.

'You're too mean to be a fairy,' Ella whispers.

'Don't call me mean!' cries Millie. Then, to everyone's surprise, Millie bursts into tears.

Chapter Five

Everyone is shocked, especially Ella. She didn't plan to make Millie cry. The class is silent. Everyone feels bad.

'Are you OK, Millie?' Ella asks.

'Sniff, sniff', goes Millie. Now Ella feels really terrible. Millie's eyes are a little bit red. Her nose is

a little bit runny and pink.
'Don't call me mean,' Millie
says in a little voice.
Nobody likes to be called
names.
'I'm sorry,' says Ella.
'I don't have any friends at
all,' says Millie.
'I thought you had lots of
friends,' says Ella.
'I did at my old school,'
says Millie. 'But I don't
know anyone here!'

Zoe and Ella look at each other. They shimmy over on their beanbag. 'Come and share with us,' they say. Millie looks at the girls. She is sick of being the new girl. It is time for Millie to make new friends. Millie plonks down on the beanbag. It is a bit squishy, but somehow they all fit. Then Mr Williams continues reading the story.

Too soon, the story is finished. The princess rides the dragon into the sunset. The fairy lives happily ever after with the princess and the dragon.

'Time to go back to your desks!' says Mr Williams.

This time, Ella and Millie put their pencil cases next to each other. The girls are going to write about what they did in the holidays.

'You can use my favourite orange pencil,' Millie says.
'You can borrow my purple pencil,' says Ella.
'Here's my best green one,' says Zoe.

The girls begin writing
their holiday stories.
'I went to the beach!' says
Zoe. She draws a sandy
beach and some waves.
'I collected some shells and
paddled in the water. Will
just laid on his towel the
whole time, reading.'

'Olivia and I went on the slip-and-slide!' Ella says. Daddy made them a slip-and-slide in the backyard. Ella had a very sore tummy after that. So did Daddy. But it was lots of fun!

'I didn't do anything exciting,' says Millie. 'Why not?' asks Ella. Holidays should be at least a little bit exciting! 'Did you go to the movies?' Millie shakes her head. 'Did you read a good book?' asks Zoe. Millie shakes her head again. 'We moved house,' Millie says. 'I used to live in the country. We even had a goat and some chickens.'

Millie draws a picture of
a big house. It has three
windows at the top and big
trees around it.

'Where do you live now?'
asks Ella.

'I live in the city now,'
Millie says. Her new
picture is of another house
with just one tree. 'My dad
changed jobs so we had
to move,' she says. 'All my
things are in boxes.'

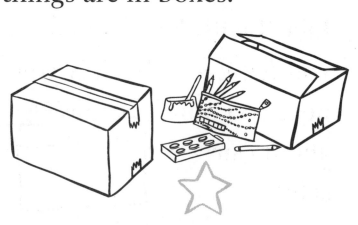

Ella and Zoe feel sorry for Millie now. It must be hard to live in a new place! Millie's stuff is packed away. She has a new bed in a new bedroom. Starting at a new school must be hard.

'Don't worry,' says Ella. 'I will show you **EVERYTHING** you need to know about our school.'

'Maybe you can play netball with us,' Zoe says. Millie has a big smile on her face. It is the first time she has smiled in ages. 'I used to play netball at my old school,' Millie says. Already she feels much better.

Ella, Zoe and their new friend, Millie, finish their holiday stories.

Next, they are going to write some new ones **TOGETHER!**

Puppy Trouble

By
Yvette Poshoglian

Illustrated by
Danielle McDonald

Chapter One

Ella and Olivia are sisters. Ella is seven years old. Olivia is five-and-a-half years old. Both girls go to big school together. Ella loves to play netball and Olivia loves to draw.

Ella and Olivia are jumping with excitement. For the last month, they have been counting down the days.

The calendar has lots of
large crosses on it.

'Only three days left, Olivia!'
says Ella.

'I can't wait!' Olivia puts an
'X' on the calendar.

Her handwriting is now very neat since she started school. On the weekend, the sisters are going to the pet shop to choose their puppy. They have wanted a dog FOREVER. Ella and Olivia will love their puppy and spoil him rotten! Maybe even more than they spoil Max. Their brother Max is only one-and-a-half years old. He has just learned to walk and is starting to talk.

Soon he won't stop talking. Ella and Olivia also love to talk. *Chatterboxes,* Mum calls them.

'You have to look after your puppy,' warns Dad. 'I'm going to take him for walks every day,' Ella promises.

'I'm going to scratch his tummy,' says Olivia. '**WOOF, WOOF**,' barks Max. Olivia leans over and gives Max a scratch on the tummy. The house is going to be very busy once the puppy arrives!

The girls work hard to get everything ready. Mum and Dad want them to look after the puppy properly, like big girls.

'The puppy will need lots of  water,' reminds Mum.

'Puppies also need lots of playtime,' Dad says. 'I've been saving this old tennis ball for you.' Dad hands Ella a stinky old tennis ball.

'Yuck!' says Ella. 'I'm going to buy our puppy a new ball!' She has been saving up her pocket money.

Finally, the calendar is full of crosses.
'No more days to cross off, Ella,' says Olivia. 'We're off to the pet shop!'
'Ready, girls?' Dad asks.
He has put towels down on the back seat of the car.

'Puppies can get very excited when they meet new people,' says Mum. 'That's why we have to put newspaper on the floor and towels in the car. Puppies are brand-new dogs. They still have to learn how to do everything. Puppies need to be toilet-trained.'

Ella and Olivia can't wait to get to the pet shop.

PET SHOP

When they arrive, they rush to the window. There are all sorts of animals and people in there. There are babies looking at tropical fish.

There are grannies looking at pretty kittens.

There are big brothers looking at guinea pigs.

Olivia spots the puppies in the middle of the pet shop.
'The puppies are here!' cries Olivia. 'Come and look!'

Ella sees a little white mop with ears.
'That's a Maltese terrier,' Dad says.
Olivia spies a spotty dog.
'That's a Dalmatian,' Dad says.

Please take me home
I am a
Golden Retriever
I am 9 weeks old

But then Olivia and Ella
see the most perfect dog in
the world. He is sitting in
the corner all by himself.

He has yellow-white fur.
His blonde eyelashes are
very long. His black nose
is soft and wet. He looks
at Ella and Olivia with his
big, brown eyes.
'We have found our puppy!'
the girls cry.

Chapter Two

On the way home, the little puppy curls up on Olivia's lap. He shivers slightly. He is a bit scared. Right now, he is tiny enough to hold in two hands. But soon enough he is going to grow into a big, strong and very fluffy dog!

'There, there,' says Olivia.

'Don't be afraid. We are
going to become best
friends!' The puppy's fur
is soft and shiny. His little
eyelashes are so beautiful.
Olivia has never seen
anything so PRECIOUS.

Ella holds a new ball that she bought at the pet shop with her pocket money. It squeaks when squeezed. It is a present for the puppy.

SQUEAK!

SQUEAK!

SQUEAK!

'Ella!' cries Dad.
'I'm just practising, Dad,' Ella says.

Together, they also bought a dog brush, a leash, a water bowl and some special puppy food.

When they get home, they let the puppy into the backyard. The puppy is not sure what to do. So he sits on the grass. He looks around. His little black nose twitches in the air.

This is his new home.
Then **ZOOM!** He is off and
racing. He sniffs the roses.

He licks the fence. He
inspects the clothes line.

Mum falls in love with the
puppy straight away.

'He is adorable!' gushes Mum. 'I love golden retrievers.'

'They are smart and funny, and very loyal,' nods Dad.

'*Ruff!*' barks Max.

The puppy spends the afternoon exploring. He disappears into the shed. He crawls under the garden hose. He even tries to bark.

'*Woof!*' goes the puppy. Then he sees a bird in a tree.

WOOF! WOOF! WOOF!

'What are we going to call him?' Olivia asks.

'Well, he is a *Golden Retriever*. What about *GR*eg?' says Mum.

'What about *GR*aham?' suggests Dad.

'You can't call a dog Graham!' says Mum.

But Ella has an idea.
'I think we should call him Bob,' says Ella. Everyone looks at the puppy.

'Bob!' Ella calls softly. The
puppy stops mid-sniff. He
turns to look at Ella.

'BOB!' Ella cries. Then she rushes over to give him a big hug.

'I think we have a dog called Bob,' laughs Dad.

The girls need to feed Bob. Puppies eat **A LOT!** They also poop a lot. Ella taps on the can with her spoon. Bob ignores her. But as soon as she puts the food in his bowl, he trots over, nose twitching.

SNIFF  SNIFF

Everything he does is so cute. Olivia fills up his water bowl. Together, they watch him eat and drink.

'I'm very proud of you, girls,' says Dad. 'But don't forget to clear out everything in the laundry. That is where Bob is going to sleep.'

'Looking after a puppy is a lot of hard work,' Mum reminds them. Ella and Olivia look at each other. They think having a puppy is really easy!

Chapter Three

When it is time to go to bed, Ella and Olivia give Bob special cuddles. Already, he is a very SPOILED puppy.

'Good night, Bob,' Ella whispers.

'Sweet dreams, Bob,' Olivia says softly.

Bob looks at them with his big, brown eyes. They take him to the laundry, where he will sleep tonight.

Ella and Olivia cover the floor with pieces of old newspaper, just in case Bob has an accident.

Bob has his own little dog bed to sleep on. It is just his size. Bob sniffs around the laundry until he finds his bed. He puts one paw on the bed, then another. Then he jumps up and finds a comfortable spot.

Soon, Bob is snoring little puppy snores. His little blonde eyelashes don't even flutter. It has been a big day with his new family. He is a tired puppy.

In the morning, the girls leap out of bed. They can't wait to see Bob!

But when Ella opens the laundry door, she gets a big shock. The laundry is such a mess. The clothes have been pulled out of the laundry basket and thrown around the room. A pair of ugg boots has been ripped to pieces. Bob's new bed has fluff spilling out of it.

Water from his bowl is sloshed across the floor. And Bob's paw prints are everywhere! Bob sits in the middle of the mess, waggling his tail.

'*Woof!*' he says. He looks very pleased with himself. 'Uh-oh,' Ella says. Bob has been very naughty! But he's only little and he hasn't been taught not to rip things up yet.

'What happened here, Bob?' Olivia asks. Then she can't resist giving him another special cuddle. So does Ella.

Mum and Dad are not amused. The laundry is a complete mess!

'Not my ugg boots, Bob!' Dad moans, holding up a half-chewed boot. 'That was my favourite pair!'

Ella and Olivia go red.
They did not get things
ready before Bob went
to bed. Ella and Olivia were
supposed to put everything
away. They *completely forgot.*

'Do you know what this means, girls?' Mum says in her serious voice. 'Bob is your puppy. He is your responsibility. You have to clean up after him.'

Ella and Olivia groan.
'But I want to play with Bob,' says Ella.
'Me too,' says Olivia.

'You can play with Bob once you have cleaned up

his mess,' Dad says. 'That's part of the job of having a new puppy.'

Ella and Olivia grumble. Bob has been quite disgusting. They pick up the clothes and put them in the washing machine. Ella gets a mop and cleans up Bob's paw prints. Olivia picks up the fluff from the ugg boots and throws it in the bin.

'Bob, you are a messy boy!'
Olivia says. Bob looks at
them with his brown eyes.
'Awwww, Bob, we can't be
stern with you for long,'
Ella laughs.
'Let's go and play, boy!'
cry Ella and Olivia.

Chapter Four

Ella and Olivia try to teach Bob to go fetch, but he's not very good at it. When they throw the ball, he runs after it, but he doesn't give it back. Bob hangs onto the ball and runs around with it in his mouth. It just fits.

Ella, Olivia and Dad take Bob for his first walk. Bob

doesn't want to wear a leash. But he does want to stop and sniff everything on the street.

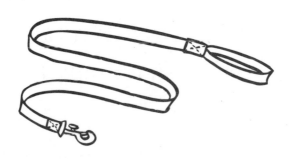

'Hold onto the leash tightly,' Dad says. 'That way he will learn what to do.' Bob is pulling left and right. He doesn't want to walk in a straight line.

'Bob wants to stop and smell the roses,' says Dad. 'This way, Bob,' says Olivia helpfully.

Ella is having a hard time
getting Bob to walk down
the footpath.
He keeps tugging her in all
sorts of directions!
He is only a little puppy,
but he is very strong.
'Be a good boy, Bob!' she
cries.

Bob stops to sniff under Mr Macpherson's gate. Mr Macpherson is their neighbour. He doesn't like animals much. Or people. Ella and Olivia are a bit scared of him.

'There's nothing there, Bob!' Ella stamps her foot. She has had enough. Bob has a lot to learn about going for a walk.
'Here you go, Olivia.'

But just as Ella hands Olivia the leash, Bob sniffs hard. Then he **TAKES OFF!** The leash slips through both Olivia's and Ella's hands.

Oh no, Bob has escaped!

'BOB!' Ella cries.

'BOB! Come back!' shouts Dad.

'BOB! **BOB! BOB!'** Olivia yells.

But it is too late. Bob scampers swiftly over Mr Macpherson's lawn and runs under the sprinkler. Droplets of water cling to his fur as he runs up the front steps of the house. The front door is wide open. Bob shakes the water off his coat and disappears inside.

Ella and Olivia spring into action. Ella climbs over the gate and Olivia follows her. Dad shakes his head and pushes it open. *Ella and Olivia have a LOT to learn about dogs and gates,* thinks Dad.

Ella and Olivia race across the lawn and through the sprinkler. They shake themselves off at Mr Macpherson's front door, just like Bob.

'We're coming in, Mr Macpherson,' cries Ella.
She is a bit scared. There is no reply. She steps through the door and into the dark hallway. There is no sign of Bob inside.
Olivia calls softly to Bob.
'Where are you, boy?'
Just when the girls are about to give up, they see Bob run out of a bedroom up ahead. His leash trails after him.

'There he is!' points Ella.
'We've got to get him!'

Together Ella and Olivia
scramble down the hallway.
Bob's leash is getting
further away.

Suddenly, they find themselves standing in Mr Macpherson's kitchen. There are pots and pans hanging from the ceiling. They can smell toast and jam. Sitting at a small table is Mr Macpherson. He has grey hair, little wire spectacles and white, woolly eyebrows.

'Is this who you are looking for?' he smiles.

Chapter Five

Bob is sitting on Mr
Macpherson's lap,
nibbling on some toast
and jam. He looks very
comfortable, and so does
Mr Macpherson.

'*Woof!*' says Bob when he
sees the two girls.

'Phew!' say Ella and Olivia.
They are very happy to
see Bob!

'Sit down, girls,' Mr Macpherson waves them in. 'Have some toast.'

Mr Macpherson strokes Bob's fur. 'This dog here is a good boy,' he says. 'He jumped up onto my lap straight away.'

'Really?' Dad asks, arriving in the kitchen.

He is surprised to see everyone eating toast. Including Bob.

'He ran away,' says Ella.
'Too quickly for us,'
adds Olivia.
Mr Macpherson looks
thoughtfully at Bob.
'How old did you say this
puppy is?' he asks.
'Nine weeks old,' says Ella.
'He is a golden retriever.'
'Golden retrievers are very
good dogs. But when they
are this young, you have
to train them,' says Mr
Macpherson.

'You have to be very firm with puppies. Otherwise they will never learn how to do things the right way.'

Olivia puts down her toast and picks up Bob's leash. Bob's training needs to start right away. 'Come on, Bob. Time to go home!'

Ella, Olivia and Dad wave
goodbye to Mr Macpherson.

Olivia is in charge of walking Bob home.

'Come on, Bob,' she says FIRMLY. 'Let's go home.' All the way home, Bob is a good boy. He sniffs only a few flowers. He chomps only a few beetles. Olivia holds onto the leash very tightly. Soon, Bob gets the hang of walking down the street. When they get back home, they take his leash off.

Bob is already off on his next big adventure. He rips through the house, and roars out into the garden. This time, he is safe in the backyard. He can't go missing there!

'We nearly lost Bob,' Ella says in a small voice. She is very glad they found him. 'Yes, I was worried sick!' Olivia blurts out.

It has been a big weekend, and Ella and Olivia have learned many new things. The two girls will get better at taking Bob for his walks and cleaning the laundry.

They also want to teach Bob good manners and new tricks. They are going to teach him how to play fetch, roll over and shake hands.

'Well done, girls!' smiles Mum, hugging them both. 'I am very proud of you. It's not easy looking after a puppy.'

Ella and Olivia sigh loudly. It is time to clean up again! They hide all the shoes in the house. They put all their favourite books out of reach. They learn how to pick up Bob's poop in a special plastic bag.

They put Bob's toys away
in a basket for next time.
Ella fills up his food bowl
with dry biscuits. Olivia
plumps up the cushion on
Bob's bed.

The girls are very tired,
and so is Bob after his big
adventure. He gives Ella
and Olivia a little lick, then
jumps up on his bed. Soon
he is fast asleep, dreaming
of ugg boots and toast
and jam.

315

ella AND Olivia

The Big Sleepover

By
Yvette Poshoglian

Illustrated by
Danielle McDonald

Chapter One

Ella and Olivia are sisters.
Ella is seven years old.
Olivia is five-and-a-half
years old. They have lots
of adventures together.
They love to cook and play
dress-ups. Both girls are
very good ballet dancers.
They adore their little
brother Max, and their
puppy Bob.

Ella and Olivia go to the same school. Olivia is in kindergarten, but Ella has been going to school for two years! She is nearly an expert. She knows where all the best hiding places are.

There is a perfect tree in the playground to read under. Ella told Olivia about this place. It is their special secret.

Ella's best friend is Zoe.
Zoe has straight black hair,
brown eyes, and she loves
to chat.

Olivia doesn't have a best
friend just yet. But she has
made lots of new friends
since starting school.

Bruno, Lily, Ryan, Jessica and David are her friends. They all sit at the same table in their classroom.

Ella and Olivia love to spend time with their friends. Sometimes Mum and Dad let Ella and Olivia invite a friend to come and play at their house after school. But the girls wish their friends could stay and play for much longer!

Ella's had an idea. She wants to do something she has never done before. Ella has been begging Mum for months to have a slumber party for her special friends. 'You're too little for sleepovers,' Mum always says to Ella.

'But I'm nearly grown-up,' says Ella. Mum can't say **NO** forever. Soon she just has to agree! Ella is not little like Olivia. Ella is very responsible now that she is seven.

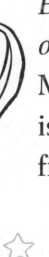

Ella is getting older, thinks Mum. Maybe it is time for Ella's first sleepover.

'Alright,' Mum finally agrees. 'You may have a friend over to stay the night at our house.' Ella doesn't have to think for very long. 'Zoe,' Ella says straight away, clapping her hands together.

Ella is so excited. Zoe and Ella will sleep in sleeping bags, have a midnight feast and stay up all night talking!

They will sleep in the lounge room, like big girls, away from everyone else! 'Can I have a sleepover, too?' Olivia asks Mum. She wants to do everything that Ella does.

'Not yet, Olivia,' Mum says.
'One sleepover at a time.'
Olivia is a teeny bit grumpy.
She wants to invite Lily,
Bruno, Ryan, Jessica and
David over for her very
own slumber party.

Ella goes to her
room and gets out
her coloured pencils,
glitter and some
paper. Zoe's invitation has
to be perfect.

Dear Zoe,

You are invited to a BIG sleepover at my house next Saturday night!

Bring your pyjamas.

There will be a midnight feast!

Love from Ella

Ella seals the invitation in an envelope. She writes Zoe's name on the front. Ella can't wait to deliver the letter in person to her best friend tomorrow at school. This is going to be the best sleepover ever!

Chapter Two

The next day, Ella slides the invitation over to Zoe's desk. Ella and Zoe sit next to each other in class. Zoe opens the card. Her eyes widen in surprise.

'A sleepover?' she says.
'I didn't think you were allowed!'

'Mum finally said **YES**,' Ella says. 'Now that we are big girls, we can have a big sleepover!'

'A midnight feast?' Zoe asks, reading on. She can't believe it. 'It's going to be so much fun!'

'Girls!' says Mr Williams, their teacher.

Those two girls are very chatty today, he thinks. But it is time for them to do some work now. The girls get their workbooks out and their pencils ready. There will be plenty of time to talk later on.

The week passes very slowly. Ella has to do some chores before having the big sleepover.

Mum has made a list for her. They are things she must do every day!

Clean bedroom

Make bed

Feed Bob

Do homework

Practise ballet

She must tick each job off as she does them. Zoe won't be allowed to come over if they are not done. The list seems very long.

Ella sighs. She doesn't want to do any boring jobs! Practising her ballet is the only thing she really wants to do. But she must do everything on the list if she wants to have the BIG sleepover on Saturday.

'C'mon, Bob!' she calls.
Ella wants to get her jobs
done early. It's time to be
a cleaning queen. Bob runs
in from the backyard. He is
here to help! Bob sniffs in
corners and snuffles under
the bed.

Ella makes her bed
very neatly. Her purple
bedspread has big pink
flowers on it.
She lines up her favourite
dolls and toys on the shelf.
She puts away all her books
on the shelf, too.

Ella glances over at Olivia's bedroom across the hall. Her bed is unmade, and her toys are everywhere. There are stacks of picture books on her bedside table.
What a baby! Ella thinks. She will NEVER be allowed to have a sleepover!

Bob follows Ella into the bathroom, where she puts on her leotard and stands at the towel rail.

'*Un*,' Ella says, moving into first position. It means 'one' in French. Her ballet teacher Mrs Fry taught her how to count to ten in French.

'Woof!' says Bob.

'*Deux*.' That means 'two' in French.

'Woof, woof!' says Bob.

'*Trois*.' Ella moves into third position.

'Woof, woof, woof!' Bob really is a very clever dog.

After ballet practice, Ella
feeds Bob. Then she does
her homework, just like
Mum asked her to.
'Well done, Ella,' Mum says.
Phew, Ella thinks.
Only four more days to go
until the big sleepover!

Chapter Three

For the rest of the week, Ella does her jobs very well. They keep her busy. As Saturday gets nearer, she prepares for the slumber party. Everything has to be just right. Ella and Dad hunt for the sleeping bags and camping gear in the shed. The shed is dark and full of cobwebs. Ella can hardly see anything.

There is so much STUFF in there!

'How do you find anything in here, Dad?' asks Ella. The shed bulges full of rakes and brooms, hammers and saws, bikes and old paint cans.

'I know where EVERYTHING is in here,' Dad says happily. 'Here we go!'

He pulls out a sleeping bag from a dark corner of the shed. An old basketball bounces down onto his head. Dad pulls out another sleeping bag. This time, two footballs and a tennis racquet topple out.

'Third one for luck,' Dad says, pulling out yet another sleeping bag.

Ping-pong balls fly out and
scatter everywhere.
'We don't need three
sleeping bags!' Ella says.
'Just in case,' Dad says,
trying to close the shed
door behind him. 'It's
getting a bit full in there,'
he admits, pushing the
door shut at last.

Dad and Ella lay the sleeping bags in the sun to air them out. Bob tries to snuggle inside one of them. 'No, Bob!' Ella cries. The sleeping bags should be a doggy-free-zone.

Ella does not want Zoe's sleeping bag to smell like Bob!

Olivia helps Ella change the pillowcases. Mum will let Ella and Zoe sleep in the lounge room if they can behave themselves.

'You're so lucky,' Olivia keeps saying.

Ella just smiles at Olivia. Sometimes it is good to be the **BIG** sister!

Ella and Olivia spend the rest of Saturday afternoon getting things ready. Zoe will arrive soon. Olivia can't wait. Olivia thinks that Zoe is one of her best friends, too. Maybe Ella will let Olivia be a part of the sleepover as well?

At six o'clock, they hear the doorbell ring.

'It's Zoe!' Ella races to the door. But Olivia beats her to it! She gives Zoe a hug.

'Hi Zoe!' Ella cries, pushing in front of Olivia. 'Come and see where we are going to sleep!'

She grabs Zoe's hand and leads her away.

'Have a good time, Zoe,' her dad calls down the hallway. 'Just remember, you need to get plenty of sleep tonight.' Zoe nods. 'You have to go riding in the morning. Ella might like to come, too.'

'Cool!' says Ella. She has always wanted to ride a horse! Tomorrow she will finally get the chance.

'Bye, Dad!' Zoe yells over her shoulder.

She is very excited and just a bit nervous. This is her first night away from home, apart from when she stays with her grandparents. She rushes back to the door and gives her dad a kiss. 'See you in the morning, Dad!' she says.

Chapter Four

'This is the best sleepover I've ever been to!' Zoe says, stuffing another marshmallow into her mouth. Ella shoves two marshmallows into her own. The girls snuggle deeper into their sleeping bags. Everything about the sleepover has been perfect so far. They had a barbeque and lots of ice-cream.

Now they are ready for the night ahead.

'Good night,' Olivia says, wishing she could stay with the big girls.

'Night, Olivia,' waves Zoe.

It is getting late. Ella changes into her favourite PJs. They are white with pink ballet slippers all over them. Zoe's PJs are green with small brown ponies all over them. 'Go and brush your teeth, girls,' Mum calls to them from down the hallway. 'It's nearly time for lights out.'

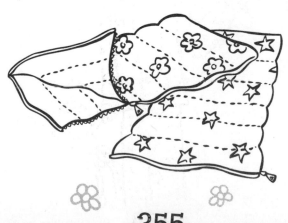

Ella and Zoe are planning a secret midnight feast. They have a torch and there is chocolate, chips and lollies. They can't wait to go to bed so they can have more fun without Mum and Dad around! The girls brush their teeth and get back into their sleeping bags.
'Good night!' say Mum and Dad together.
'Night!' the girls reply.

Then Mum turns the light
off. The room goes dark.
Zoe misses her own Mum
and Dad a tiny bit. It is a
bit strange sleeping in a
different house. Ella tries
to get comfortable. So
does Zoe. The house is
very quiet, with only Bob's
puppy snores coming from
the laundry.

Ella switches on the torch.
'Ready for a feast?'

'Yes!' Zoe whispers. The two girls fumble in the dark for some chocolate. Ella holds the torch under her chin and tells scary stories.

Soon Zoe forgets all about her worries.

'Wooooo!' Ella pretends to be a ghost. The two girls can't help laughing. Their giggles echo around the lounge room.

OH NO! They have woken someone up! Ella hopes it isn't Max.

'Shhh!' Ella says. The light in the hallway comes on. *Uh-oh*, thinks Ella.

'What are you doing?' It is Olivia. She is sleepy. Her doll, Miss Sparkle, looks sleepy, too.

'Can I stay with you?' Olivia asks.

'Sleepovers are for big girls only!' Ella whispers.

'It's OK,' says Zoe. 'Come and join us, Olivia!'

Olivia smiles and runs
to find her sleeping bag.
Then, on tip-toes, she joins
the big girls for the big
sleepover, snuggling up
between Ella and Zoe on
the couch.

'Did I miss the midnight
feast?' Olivia whispers.
'You are just in time!' Zoe
whispers back. The three
girls eat until they can't eat
any more.

'I'm tired,' Ella finally says.

'Me too,' says Zoe.

'Me too,' says Olivia.

'I think I ate too much,'
Ella says, rubbing her
tummy.
'Me too,' says Zoe.
Me too, thinks Olivia.
Soon the girls are snoring,
holding each other's sticky
hands as they sleep.

Chapter Five

The next morning, Mum walks into the lounge room. She is surprised to find not two, but three sleepyheads tucked into their sleeping bags. The girls are wrapped up tight. *What a mess,* thinks Mum. There are lolly wrappers and chip crumbs all over the floor. The place looks disgusting!

The girls even have chocolate all over their faces! 'Wakey-wakey, girls,' Mum says. Olivia snores. Zoe snuffles. Ella sighs. All three girls are fast asleep!

'Wake up, Zoe!' Mum says again. 'It's time to get up. Your dad will be here soon.' She nudges Zoe gently. Zoe finally opens her eyes. She looks at the sleeping sisters beside her. They are still snoring away! Zoe is tired, too. Perhaps they stayed up a little bit too late?

'C'mon Ella, c'mon Olivia!'
Zoe nudges the girls. It is
nearly nine o'clock!
But Ella and Olivia
don't move a muscle.
They are in dreamland.
Zoe pulls herself out of
the sleeping bag and gets
dressed. Then she brushes
her teeth.
DING! DONG!
Zoe's dad is here already!
'Did you have fun, Zoe?' her
dad asks.

'It was the best!' Zoe nods.

'I'm afraid they were up
a bit late,' Mum says. Zoe
goes red. 'It was a BIG
sleepover.'

Zoe's dad smiles. 'Is Ella
coming riding with us
today?' he asks. Zoe and
Mum look at each other.
'Ella is still asleep, I'm
afraid,' Mum says. 'She
will be very sorry that she
missed out on going riding
with you.'

'Thanks for having me,' Zoe says to Mum.
'Have fun today, Zoe!' Mum waves them goodbye. Her girls are very lazy indeed!

When Ella and Olivia finally wake up, they look for Zoe. But she has gone. Instead, they find Mum standing, with her hands on her hips. *Uh-oh*, the girls think.

'Where's Zoe?' Ella asks.

'Zoe's already gone riding,' Mum says.

'**OH NO!**' Ella cries. 'I was going to go too!' Ella is very upset. She didn't say goodbye to Zoe. Now she can't go riding with her!

'I tried to wake you up,'
Mum frowns. 'But I can see
that you were all up very
late last night.'
Ella has a funny feeling in
her tummy. She doesn't like
being in trouble.

'Maybe you're not old enough to have sleepovers?' Mum says.

'Yes I am, Mum!' Ella says. She is not going to ruin anything else. 'I promise we will clean up!'

That is how Ella and Olivia spend Sunday morning— doing the **BIG CLEAN UP** after the big sleepover.

Ella writes a list of chores for them both.

Roll sleeping bags up

Change the pillowcases

Sweep up crumbs

Tidy the lounge room

Olivia doesn't grumble once. Big girls have sleepovers, and big girls have to clean up! Ella is secretly proud of her little sister. They are cleaning queens together! And the sleepover had been a lot of fun. Zoe even rang Ella to invite her to come riding **NEXT** time!

By the time the girls are finished, the lounge room is sparkling. They even sweep the floor twice for good measure. It sure is hard work having lots of fun together!

Ella can't wait to see Zoe on Monday. Maybe it will be Zoe's turn to have the next sleepover!

eLLa AND Olivia

Pony Problem

By
Yvette Poshoglian

Illustrated by
Danielle McDonald

Chapter One

Ella and Olivia are sisters.
Ella is older than Olivia.
She is seven years old and
Olivia is five-and-a-half
years old.

The sisters have lots of
adventures together. Ella
likes to be in charge.
That's because she is the
BIG sister.

Ella and Olivia also have a little brother called Max. Max learns new words every day. His favourite words are MINE and NOW. When he is older, he will be a real chatterbox. Max will also be an adventurer, just like his big sisters.

Ella and Olivia live with Mum, Dad, Max, and their puppy, Bob.

Ella, Olivia and Max all have different shades of brown hair.

Bob has golden hair that collects in tufts all over the backyard.

'So much dog hair, so little time!' Mum always says.

Zoe has come to visit this afternoon. Zoe is Ella's best friend. She has black hair and brown eyes. Zoe loves horseriding and playing netball. Zoe thinks Olivia is fun to play with, too.

Sometimes, Zoe wishes she had a little sister, just like Ella does. Zoe has a big brother called Will. He is not at all like Olivia!

Today, Zoe and Ella are brushing Bob's coat. His fur starts to shine. Bob loves it and wags his tail like he always does when people brush his coat.

'I am taking part in an equestrian competition on the weekend,' Zoe tells Ella and Olivia.

Equestrian means something to do with horses. They think Zoe is lucky to have a horse and go riding on the weekends. It must be fun to trot around on such a beautiful animal. Ella is a teeny bit jealous that Zoe has a horse, but she tries not to show it.

'Would you like to come and watch my event?' Zoe asks. It would make her and Hattie very happy. Hattie is Zoe's horse.

She is a beautiful filly with a chestnut coat. A filly is a girl horse. With Ella and Olivia cheering her on, they might just be able to win the competition! Zoe hopes to win first prize in her event on the weekend.

Ella missed out on seeing the stables last time. She has been waiting for another chance to visit them with Zoe.

'I would **LOVE** to come to the competition,' Ella cries.
'Me too,' Olivia says.
'I can't wait to see Hattie!' Ella says.

The sisters are very excited that they will be able to spend so much time with all the sleek horses and clever ponies.

The equestrian event is on Saturday. Zoe will train first and then compete in her event. Hattie will need to be brushed and prepared for competition.

Both the horses and the riders will be judged on the day.

Ella and Olivia ask Mum
if they can go to the event
with Zoe.

'Of course,' says Mum. 'But
you must be careful around

the animals.'
The girls nod.
'Yes, Mum!'
they say.
They can't
wait until
Saturday
arrives.

Chapter Two

'How do I look?' Ella asks Olivia. It is finally the weekend. Ella wears cream leggings and a tie. Olivia wears jeans, just in case she gets to ride a pony!

Ella has her gumboots on. She pretends that they are riding boots, like the ones Zoe wears and keeps in a special box.

'We're both wearing our riding clothes,' Olivia says. She wishes she had some boots, too. She only has her old sandshoes on!

Zoe and her family arrive early on Saturday morning to pick up Ella and Olivia. Zoe's car has a horse trailer attached to it. From the back, they can see Hattie. Their pony, Jett, is also in the trailer. They have just picked the horse and pony up from their stables.

Jett and Hattie wear special rugs over them to keep them warm.

Zoe wears her special
riding outfit. She has cream
jodhpurs on. They are the
special pants that all the
riders wear.

Her red blazer is very swish.
Her ponytail is tied back
with a ribbon. She wears
long brown boots, nearly up
to the knee.

When Zoe rides in
competitions she wears a
helmet with a chinstrap in
case she falls off.

Ella and Olivia pile into the car. They are finally on their way to the equestrian centre! When they arrive, they have flutters in their tummies.

There are so many horses and quite a few ponies. Riders of all ages prance around in their special outfits. Everyone is busy preparing for their competition!

The loudspeaker crackles with announcements. Zoe looks at her watch.

'Hattie and I have to go now,' Zoe says to the girls. She takes Hattie's reins and rubs her gently on the flank. Beside them, Jett swishes his tail. He wants to be in the competition, too!

'You can give Hattie a pat,' Zoe says. Ella puts her hand out and gently rubs Hattie's soft hair.

She is such a beautiful horse. But Olivia is a bit frightened. Up close, Hattie is so big. She is a little bit afraid to touch her.

'Don't be frightened, Olivia,' says Ella. She takes Olivia's hand in hers and together they give Hattie a pat with soft strokes. Somehow Olivia feels brave with Ella next to her.

'Good luck!' Olivia says.
Ella gives Zoe a quick hug.
Zoe leads Hattie away.

'We'll be looking out for you!' Ella calls out.

But before Ella can walk up to the stand with Olivia, a busy-looking lady with a clipboard bustles over. The lady looks at Ella in her strange riding outfit. Then she looks at Jett, who is still swishing his tail.

'Young lady, you are late for the pony competition!' she says. 'It starts in five minutes!' Before Ella can say anything, the lady plonks a helmet on her head and ties up the chinstrap. She grabs hold of Jett's reins.

'Follow me,' the lady says. Ella is nervous and excited. Could this be her big chance to ride a pony?

Chapter Three

The lady walks Jett and
Ella to a marshalling area.
There are plenty of ponies
and riders milling around.
Everyone looks serious.
They all want to win their
competitions! Ella looks
up to the stands. She sees
Olivia sitting with Will and
Zoe's parents. Ella hopes that
nobody notices that she is
wearing gumboots!

'Up you get,' says the
lady, helping Ella into
Jett's saddle. Jett is very
calm, but Ella is very
NERVOUS! She's never
been on a pony before.

She holds on tight to the reins. She doesn't want to fall off. Jett trots slowly over to the competition yard.

Ella can see a lot from up here! The other ponies are lovely, but not as nice as Jett with his shiny black coat. She hopes Jett is having as much fun as she is! She starts to get used to the rhythm of Jett walking slowly.

As long as he doesn't go too fast, Ella thinks. *Then everything should be fine.*

Up in the stands, Olivia looks for Zoe and Hattie. As she gazes around, she is SHOCKED by what she sees. Is that really Ella riding Jett in the pony competition?

Ella doesn't even know how to ride, thinks Olivia. Olivia is worried. She doesn't want Ella to fall off and hurt herself!

Olivia leaps up. It is time to save her sister. Thank goodness she wore her sandshoes!

She runs down to the marshalling area for the horses. She looks and looks. Finally, she spies Zoe. 'Zoe!' she cries. '**ZOE!!!!**'

Zoe and Hattie are nearly ready for the competition. Zoe is nervous, but she might just come first, second or third! She has been training for the competition for quite a long time.

Just as Hattie reaches the gate, Zoe hears a voice calling for her. She turns to see Olivia calling out over the fence.

'Zoe! Come here,' Olivia cries. Zoe gently pulls on the reins and steers Hattie over to Olivia.

'Is everything OK?' she asks. Olivia shakes her head.

'Ella and Jett . . .' she says.

'What?' Zoe asks.

Olivia points over to the ponies and their riders.

'Ella is on Jett! And they are about to go into the competition!' she cries.

Zoe looks around. To her amazement, she can see Ella sitting on Jett. Ella looks a little bit worried.

'Oh dear, I must go and save her!' she says to Olivia. 'She doesn't know how to ride properly!' Zoe knows how much Ella loves ponies, but ponies can be dangerous if you don't know how to ride.

'Olivia, go and tell Will and Mum and Dad where Ella is,' Zoe cries over her shoulder. Olivia springs into action.

Olivia is very proud of Zoe. Zoe is such a good friend that she will go and help Ella. *Poor Zoe*, thinks Olivia. *She is about to miss her own competition!*

Chapter Four

Zoe forgets all about her competition. She has to save Ella! Jett is a good pony, but Zoe doesn't want Ella to fall off. She might hurt herself. Zoe fell off a pony when she was a little girl. It was very painful. Understanding ponies and horses takes time—sometimes they don't like strangers riding them!

Zoe trots over to the edge of the competition yard where all the ponies and their riders are.

'Ella!' she cries. **ELLAAAA!**

But Ella can't hear her. Ella is too busy holding on for dear life. She and Jett are about to begin their own event! This day has been scary, but exciting so far.

Ella watches the other riders. They begin with a slow walk around the edge of the arena.
I can do that, Ella thinks. After all, she has stayed on this long!

'C'mon, Jett,' Ella whispers to the pony. 'We can do it.'

Ella doesn't hear Zoe's voice calling her from outside the arena. Then, it is too late. The lady with the clipboard leads Ella and Jett over to the arena. 'Good luck,' the lady says. Then Ella and Jett take centrestage in the arena.

For the first time, Ella is scared. There are no other riders around. Can she really do this? Everything goes quiet. Ella is quite sure that everyone in the stands can hear the thumping of her heart. She tries to be brave inside.

Ella hears a faint voice. Someone calls her name. But Ella is too scared to turn around and look.

419

Ella has to concentrate hard! She walks Jett around the edge of the arena fence like all the other ponies. Jett seems fine, but then he starts to speed up a little. *Uh-oh*, thinks Ella.

'Slow down, Jett!' she whispers.

But Jett wants to win the competition. He breaks into a slow trot, just like Zoe taught him to do.

Ella grabs the reins even more tightly. She tries not to look at the ground. Her helmet slides down her forehead. But she is too scared to push it up. Zoe can't believe what she sees! Ella and Jett are riding around the pony arena. Ella clings on tightly. There is only one thing that Zoe can do. She has to rescue her best friend!

'Are you ready for an adventure, Hattie?' Zoe whispers to the filly. Together, they push their way through the riders.

'Coming through!' she says to the lady with the clipboard. The lady looks very surprised. But Zoe is ready.

Together, Hattie and Zoe take off and head into the arena. They are trotting very quickly now. It is time to take the reins and save her friend, Ella.

Chapter Five

Ella is flying. Jett breaks into a fast trot. Ella grips the reins even tighter. She had no idea that ponies could go so fast. But Ella wants to get off Jett. **Right now.** She has had enough riding to last a lifetime. She feels herself sliding off to one side.

Hang on, Ella thinks to herself.

'Ella!' someone calls. The voice gets louder and louder. Ella is very surprised when she sees Zoe and Hattie ride up alongside her in the arena.

⌘

'Hold on, Ella!' Zoe cries. Then she pulls Hattie up to ride even more closely to Jett and Ella.

The horse and pony both begin to slow down. Then, to Ella's surprise, Jett comes to a stop. In the middle of the arena, Hattie and Zoe have saved the day. And Ella, too.

Zoe dismounts and slides off Hattie. Carefully, she grabs Jett's reins in her hands and slowly walks the horse and pony to the edge of the arena.

The judges run out onto the course. They are very worried about Ella and Jett.

'I think you saved your friend,' a judge says to Zoe. He is impressed with the young girl with the black ponytail. Zoe is happy that she has rescued them both. But she is worried about Ella. Ella looks a little bit frightened and pale.

'Are you alright, Ella?' asks another voice nearby.

This time, Ella does look around. Olivia's face peers over the fence.

'I'm alright,' Ella says in a little voice. She feels a little bit sick. She shouldn't have gone in the competition.

Next to Olivia, she sees the very worried faces of Zoe's parents.

'Ella, you have some explaining to do,' says Zoe's dad. He looks very serious. But then he looks at Zoe and smiles. 'Well done, Zoe,' he says. 'I am very proud of you. You have done very well to help Ella and Jett.'

Zoe beams. Even though she missed her competition, Zoe knows it was important to help Ella. She knows there will be many more chances to come.

The judges help Ella dismount. She is happy to be back on solid ground. Ella rushes to give Zoe a big thankyou hug.
'You are the best friend in the world!' she says.

'Don't thank me,' Zoe says. 'Thank Olivia. She was the one who really saved you!' Ella gives Olivia a hug, too.

Olivia is glad that her big sister is safe and sound. Thank goodness she didn't fall off!

It is nearly time to go. Ella gives Jett a final pat. 'Thanks for the ride,' Ella whispers. It is probably going to be a **LOOOONG** time before she ever goes riding again!

But before they leave the arena, the lady with the clipboard rushes up to Zoe. 'You can't leave yet,' she says. 'You must wait for the winners to be announced. Come with me.'

Zoe holds on to Hattie's reins and follows the lady. She feels a little bit sad inside that she will not be a winner today.

All the prize-winners
gather on a special stand in
the middle of the arena.
The judges are standing
next to a table
with prize
ribbons for
the riders.

There are blue ribbons for first place. There are red ribbons for second, and yellow for third. There is a very special purple ribbon to be awarded.
It is for Zoe.

The lady with the clipboard beams as she pins the ribbon to Zoe's jacket. 'Congratulations,' she says to Zoe.

Zoe looks down at her ribbon, it says 'Best and Fairest'.

This is the best award of all! Zoe thinks. Ella and Olivia clap and cheer. Well done, Zoe!

439

By
Yvette Poshoglian

Illustrated by
Danielle McDonald

Chapter One

Ella and Olivia are sisters. Ella is seven years old and has a long brown ponytail. Olivia is five-and-a-half years old and has freckles on her nose.

Ella and Olivia have a little brother called Max. Max loves to hide his sisters' toys!

Ella and Olivia are crazy.
Crazy for **Cool Kitties!**
They want to own the
whole collection. Cool
Kitties are very special toys.
Cool Kitties are pets that
don't need to be walked or
brushed, or fed.

The sisters already have a
real pet. They have a golden
retriever called Bob. He is
still a puppy.

They take Bob for walks,
play with him and brush
his thick coat. One real dog
is enough for now.

Ella and Olivia play with their Cool Kitties for hours. Everyone at their school collects them, too! Cool Kitties come in all colours and sizes. Best of all, they fit into your pocket.

'Zoe has sixteen Cool Kitties,' Ella exclaims. She wants even more Cool Kitties than Zoe.
'I want to own the whole set,' she says.

That is a big job. There are over fifty to collect!

'I have eight Cool Kitties,' Olivia says proudly. She lines them up on her bedside table. There is a white Kitty, a brown Kitty and a tabby cat. Her favourite Kitty is purple with a small pink crown on its ears.

Together, the girls have fifteen Cool Kitties. That means Ella has seven Kitties. Olivia owns more than Ella does!

'I want to buy more Kitties,' Ella says. She can be very bossy when she wants something.

'Do you have any money, Olivia?' she demands.

'No,' Olivia says in a small voice. Then she speaks up. 'Do you, Ella?'

Ella shakes her head. Her piggy bank is empty. Her purse has no coins in it at all! She can't find any coins on the floor, in her drawers or in her pockets.

'Let's ask Dad to buy us some more,' Ella says. 'Good idea!' Olivia agrees. Dad spoils the girls all the time! They find him vacuuming in the lounge room.

'Ouch!' he says. He always seems to step on a Cool Kitty. They are everywhere! Dad is getting a bit sick of the Kitties.

There is a loud, clanging noise coming from inside the vacuum cleaner. 'Whoops!' Dad says. 'There goes a Cool Kitty!' **OH NO!** Dad just vacuumed up a Kitty, never to be seen again.

'You must put your toys away, girls,' Dad says. 'Otherwise, you will lose them.'

Ella and Olivia are very worried. Until they rescue the lost Kitty, they only have fourteen Cool Kitties! Because she is the big sister, Ella takes charge. This is a very serious matter.

'Dad,' she begins. 'We need some more Cool Kitties!' Olivia nods her head.

Dad opens the vacuum cleaner and pulls out the lost Kitty. Then he turns to the girls. 'You girls need to earn some pocket money,' he says. And then, because Ella is the big sister, he hands her the vacuum cleaner. 'Maybe you can start now?'

Chapter Two

Ella and Olivia are busy cleaning all weekend. Ella vacuums, and Olivia tidies her bedroom. They help Mum clean the fridge. It is a little bit disgusting. 'Hmmm . . . pickle juice!'

Mum says, holding up a jar with green juice. 'Squashed tomatoes!' It is a yucky job. But the girls want to earn lots of pocket money to buy more Cool Kitties.

'I didn't expect you girls to help me,' Mum says. Ella and Olivia have been very useful around the house. Mum is a bit PUZZLED.

'Just being little helpers,' Ella says. She gives Olivia a secret smile.

By the time they get into bed on Sunday night, they are very tired.

'I think we earned lots of money this weekend,' Olivia murmurs to Ella from across the hall. 'We can buy thirty-six Kitties for sure!'

But all she can hear is snoring! Ella is fast asleep, dreaming of the new Kitties that she will put on her bedside table.

The next day, there is some bad news. The girls have hardly earned any pocket money at all!

Dad says they need to work for a lot longer than a weekend to earn their pocket money.

'At least a week,' he says to Ella and Olivia. 'The more you do, the more you earn.' But he puts a few coins into their piggy banks to start them off.

Ella and Olivia still can't buy any more Kitties. They are going to have to try even harder around the house. Even though it is boring to do chores, it looks like they are going to have to do them! They *must* complete their Cool Kitties collection.

At school, everyone plays with their Kitties at recess and lunchtime. Zoe brings her favourites to school. She brings her top ten! They barely fit into her pockets!

Sometimes, the girls swap Cool Kitties for ones they like more. Ella traded a dull, brown Kitty for a cool, sparkly Kitty last week. It was a good trade!

Mr Williams is on duty. He doesn't understand the Cool Kitties craze. 'When I was your age, we read books or played at recess and lunchtime!' He shakes his head. Ella frowns. She likes to read *and* play with Cool Kitties. She just can't do both at the same time.

'I'm saving up for more,'
Ella says to her friends.
'I had to save up for AGES,'
says Millie. Millie is Ella's
new friend. Millie has the
biggest collection. She has
a special carry-case that
holds all her Cool Kitties.
Ella wants one just like
it. Maybe she will earn
enough money to buy that
carry-case, too.

'How long did you save for?' asks Ella.

'Over a month,' Millie says.

A MONTH? Ella knows that she is going to have to work very hard. Maybe even harder than Olivia! But it will be worth it in the end when she lines up her Cool Kitties in her new case!

Chapter Three

Olivia is also very keen to earn some pocket money. When she gets home, she checks in on her collection. Phew! They are all there. Her Cool Kitties have been waiting for her! She counts her Kitties. One, two, three, four, five, six, seven, eight— cute as a button. She looks at Ella's. She has seven Kitties.

Olivia is already ahead of her big sister!

Before they start their chores, the girls get their coloured pencils out and some paper to create a chart.

JOB	Ella	Olivia
♡ Playing with Bob		
☆ Drying the dishes		
❀ Cleaning lounge room		
☁ Helping with laundry		
◇ Feeding Bob		
❀ Setting the table		

The chart will help them keep track of everything they do around the house. Mum and Dad have promised them a whole dollar for each job done. Soon they will have enough money to get as many Cool Kitties as they like.

Mum puts the chart on the fridge. She is proud of her girls for having such a good plan.

Olivia's first job is to play with Bob.

'Fetch, boy!' she calls. Bob runs off in search of his favourite tennis ball. He still hasn't learned to give it back, though.

He drops the soggy tennis ball on the grass and runs back to Olivia, tail wagging.

This is going to be easy! thinks Olivia.

Inside, Ella is tidying the lounge room. She stacks all the magazines in a neat pile. She lines up the television remotes. She sprays special glass cleaner and carefully wipes down the coffee table with a sponge. It's hard work earning money!

Outside, Olivia plays a little longer with Bob. 'Hungry?' Olivia asks Bob. Bob stops mid-run and turns around. HUNGRY is his favourite word. His tail thumps up and down. He grins from ear to ear. It's dinnertime! Olivia opens the tin of dog food and spoons it carefully into his bowl. Bob can't wait. He starts licking the spoon before it's in the dish!

Later that evening, Ella
helps Mum in the kitchen.
She mashes the potato. She
squeezes the lemon juice
for the salad. Olivia
straightens the tablecloth
and sets the table
neatly.

Her knives and forks, plates and napkins are perfect. 'I am very pleased with you two girls,' Dad beams. He and Mum are very happy with their helpful girls. The house is as neat as a pin!

Every afternoon, the girls continue with their jobs. They have to do their homework, too. Somehow they have to fit everything in. All this work hasn't left much time to play with their Cool Kitties! Ella is slightly ahead on the chart. 'I'm busier than you,' Ella says.

JOB	Ella	Olivia
♡ Playing with Bob	||	||
☆ Drying the dishes	|||	|
❀ Cleaning lounge room	||	
☁ Helping with laundry	|||	|
◇ Feeding Bob	|	||
✿ Setting the table	|||	|

'I'm working hard, too!' Olivia says. She hates it when Ella bosses her around. *I will work even harder at my chores tomorrow*, thinks Olivia. She simply has to beat Ella.

Ella grows more excited each day. She is faster at jobs than Olivia. She is going to save the most money and have even more Cool Kitties!

Chapter Four

By the end of the week, Ella and Olivia are very cross with each other. Both of them want to do the jobs. Ella is beating Olivia by a long way on their chart! Olivia hates losing.

'Need any help, Mum?' Ella always asks sweetly, just before Olivia has her chance to ask.

'Not right now, Ella,' Mum says.

Mum is a bit sick of it.

The house is clean and her wallet is empty.

Mum also doesn't like it when her two girls fight. Usually they get on like a house on fire. But they are both trying so hard to earn money that they are not getting on. Mum is completely over the Cool Kitty craziness!

'I'm going to play with Bob,' announces Ella. 'No, I am!' Olivia says.

'Stop it, girls,' Mum says. 'Neither of you are going to play with Bob. He is spoiled rotten and can spend some time on his own,' she says. 'Tomorrow we will go to the toyshop after school and you can buy your Kitties. Then we can go back to normal!' Mum never thought she would say that!

There are no more jobs to do. Ella and Olivia go to the lounge room and sit with their Kitties. Instead of playing with them, they decide to open their piggy banks. Olivia tries not to be too grumpy. Her piggy bank is very heavy. But Ella's is a bit heavier.

The girls count their money. Ella has fifteen dollars and Olivia has nine dollars.

The next morning, the girls put their Kitties in their schoolbags. Today, everyone is bringing their Kitties to school. Ella zips her schoolbag up.

Olivia is running late today. She stuffs her Kitties into the front pocket of her backpack and runs out the front door. But she forgets to zip up her bag!

When they get to school, Ella runs ahead of Olivia. There is just enough time to play with her friends before the bell goes. Olivia hates being left behind. 'Wait, Ella!' she cries. Olivia isn't looking where she is going. She stumbles and falls. Her backpack goes flying.

Ella turns around. Olivia
has fallen and scraped her
knee. Ella feels terrible. She
is supposed to hold Olivia's
hand!
'Are you alright, Olivia?'
she says, rushing to her
side. Olivia tries not to cry.
'I'm OK,' she sniffs. Ella
picks up Olivia's bag.
'Let's go to the office and
get a bandaid,' Ella says.
It is time to be a big sister
and do the right thing.

Ella carries Olivia's bag for her and holds her hand.

Olivia is very brave while
her scrapes are cleaned.
Ella waits with her and pats
her hand. Ella digs a Cool
Kitty out of her bag.
'You can look after Leo
today,' she says to Olivia.
Leo is Ella's favourite! He is
yellow with a lion's mane.
Ella puts it in Olivia's hand.
She squeezes it tight.

Chapter Five

Ella and Olivia can't wait until recess. Everyone is going to meet in the playground to line up their Kitties and play together. Finally, the bell rings.

DING-DING!

Up in Mr Williams's classroom, Ella grabs her play lunch and then her Kitty collection.

Millie, Zoe and Jo also grab their Kitties. It's time to play!

Down in the kindergarten block, Olivia grabs her apple. Leo the Kitty is still in her pocket. She feels a lot better. She looks in the front pocket of her bag. It is already open! She puts her hand inside, but it is EMPTY! Olivia tips her schoolbag upside down.

A water bottle comes tumbling out. A red pencil does, too. And worst of all, a mashed banana that Olivia has forgotten to unpack! But there is no sign of any of her Kitties.

Olivia thinks back to the morning. They must have fallen out when she tripped over! She hopes that she can find them. It took her a long time to collect those Cool Kitties.

Olivia rushes over to the playground.

'Ella!' she cries. 'ELLA!!'

Olivia pushes through the crowd of big kids. They are lining up the Kitties on a log. She has to find Ella.

She knows that her sister
will help her.

'What's wrong, Olivia?'
Suddenly, Ella is right
beside her. Already, Olivia
feels a bit better.

'All my Kitties are gone!'
she cries.
'Where are they?' Ella asks.
'I think they fell out of my
backpack this morning,'
Olivia says.

Oh dear, thinks Ella. Could
it be all her fault that
Olivia's Kitties are gone?
'I'll help you find them,'
Ella says.
'Me too,' says Millie.
'So will we,' say Zoe and Jo.

Together, the Cool Kitty fans hunt for Olivia's lost toys. They scour the playground looking for the little figurines.

'Found one!' says Millie. It is Princess Kitty, Olivia's favourite.

'Here's another!' says Jo. It is a lime green Kitty with pink spots. But as hard as they search, they can't find any of the others.

Olivia tries hard not to cry.
It is such a shame!
She used to have eight, and
now she only has two!

Ella has a brilliant idea.
'Why don't we each give
her one of our Kitties?'
she says.
Zoe, Millie, Jo and Ella
each donate a Cool Kitty
to Olivia.
Soon, Olivia nearly has as
many as when she started!
She can't stop grinning.
But if only she could find
her lost Kitties . . .

Everyone feels much better once Olivia has some Kitties to play with.

'It's lucky we're going to the toyshop this afternoon,' Olivia says. But she secretly loves her new Kitties and wouldn't trade them for the world.

That afternoon at the toyshop, Ella's and Olivia's tummies are flipping with excitement. Olivia is a bit sad that she doesn't have as much money as Ella.

'I have a great idea!' says Ella. 'Let's put all our money together and share all the Kitties!' Olivia beams. Together, the girls choose ten new Kitties!

'And this is for being so responsible,' Mum says. She places a brand-new carry-case for the girls' Kitties in front of them. It is a present from Mum and Dad. Olivia and Ella are over the moon!

Later that evening, Ella and Olivia take all of their Cool Kitties out of their new carry-case and line them up on the big table.

All their hard work this week has been worth it. Together, they have the best collection of all!

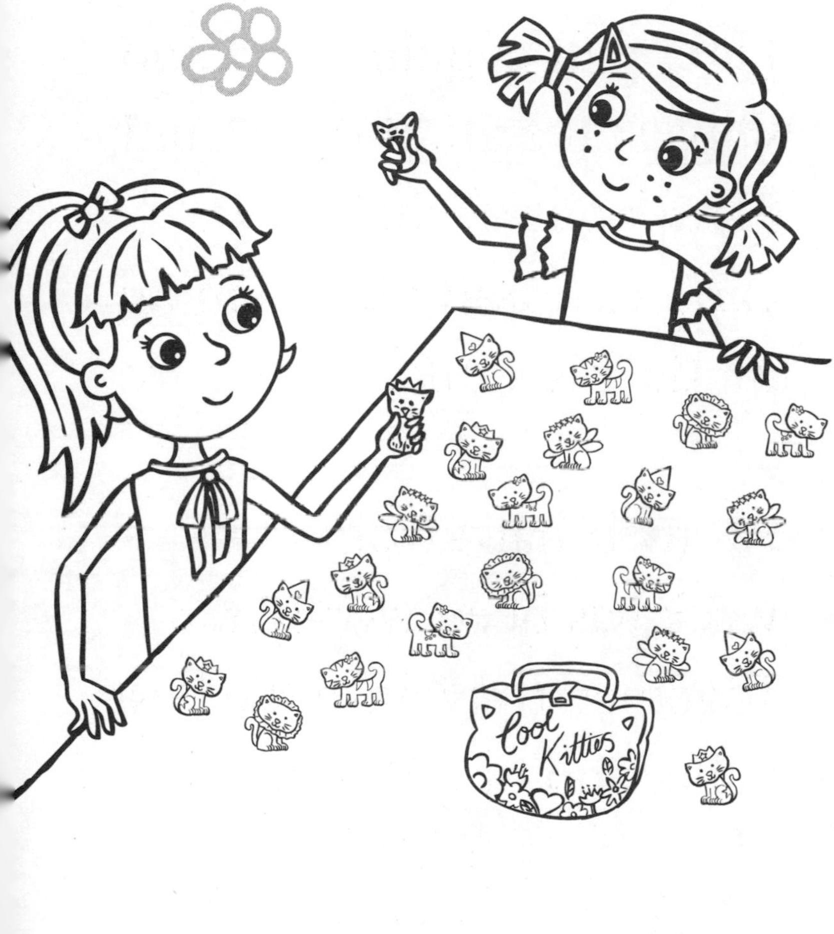
Cool Kitties

Collect
them
all!

The Christmas Surprise

Sports Carnival

Flower Power

Christmas Wonderland

Beach Holiday

Spelling Superstar

Hair Disaster

Netball Fever

Zoo Rescue